L E O N I E
G A N T

CURSE

THE

HEART

The Harstone Legacy
Book 3

ISBN-13: 978-0-9943999-7-7

To Mike, Samuel and Nicholas

"*V*oila." I slammed my greatest creation and the proof that I was finally ready to embrace my witch heritage down on the diner table in front of my closest friend.

Tilda stopped drinking her milkshake, mid-slurp.

"What is that?"

I picked it up and admired my handiwork. "It's my cone of silence spell. I've finally been able to do it. Now we don't have to use yours all the time."

"It's a troll doll."

"Your point being?"

Tilda dropped her head into her hands. "Witches are generally all about nature. That's why most people put the privacy spell on a small stone or a gem that means something to them. At worst it will be a piece of trashy jewelry. A plastic troll doll with orange hair is not a normal choice."

I picked up the inch-tall doll and activated it. "But it works. I found it while I was unpacking." I stroked its long hair. "I got this in the party favor bag at the one birthday party I was ever invited to as a child. That makes it special."

Tilda shook her head. "No, that makes it sad."

I put it in the center of the table and sat down. "Well, I'm proud of it."

"What is that thing in the middle of your table?"

I smiled as I looked up into the eyes of my Destined Beloved. I know, I can't believe it's a thing either. It does sound ridiculous, but in a paranormal town like Walker Bay, if the Seer has a Destined Beloved prophecy about you, then your soul is linked forever to another person. In my case, that other person was the sheriff of Walker Bay as well as a newly discovered berserker werewolf. We were still working out the details of our relationship.

"It's a troll doll," I said, still proud of the spell, despite Tilda's attitude.

Conall picked up my enchanted toy. "It's naked and it has weird hair, and trolls look nothing like this."

I grabbed it out of his hand and put it back on the table. "I've put a cone of silence spell on it. It's the first one that worked."

The look of confusion on Conall's face was classic and very familiar. As a person who had lived my whole life in the non-paranormal world, my cultural upbringing had been a little different to his.

"She means a privacy spell," Tilda said, the tone in her voice indicating that my lack of knowledge about all things paranormal was no longer cute and endearing.

Conall decided that discussion about the troll doll would have to end. "What are you doing today?"

I sighed. This was once again a part of the whole Destined Beloved situation. Despite originally wanting to fight the belief that we were bound by fate and couldn't change it, we had both come to the realization that there was something between us and we were going to give it a go. In the mind of a protective berserker sheriff, that meant he had to know where I was at all times to ensure I was safe. It was taking a lot longer than I thought to disabuse him of that notion.

"Well, after I have breakfast with Tilda, I was planning on taking her on a road trip where we would find her a gorgeous guy to spend a memorable afternoon with, and remind her, despite her cranky attitude today, that she's a sensual woman. Then, after doing a couple of armed robberies, we would lead law enforcement on a high-speed chase until they trapped us on the edge of a cliff. After deciding there was no way we were going to end up in jail, we were going to clasp hands, gun the engine, and sail over the edge of the cliff into eternity together."

Conall sighed in a way that indicated he was having trouble thinking of me as cute and endearing as well. "Fine, don't tell me. Just make sure you keep your phone on." He walked away, shaking his head, grabbed his order and left the diner.

"That was from a movie, right?" Tilda asked as she went back to her milkshake.

"Yeah." I smiled as the waitress glared at me while delivering my food. I had got used to the glares of the former paramours of my Destined Beloved. I really had no choice considering he had made his way through a fair number of the local female population when he was only a teenager. The only reason I was still able to eat at the diner was because I knew there was a spell over the place which made any food with a contaminant go black and rancid immediately. It meant I could be pretty sure that nobody had added anything unpleasant to my food, despite how much they might want to.

"You seem pretty happy with the world," Tilda commented.

"I am," I replied as I tucked into my omelet. "I'm getting used to the way things happen here. I know you're not impressed with my cone of silence troll doll, but it took me forever to master that spell. I'm pretty sure Flora was ready to give up on me and find a remedial class she could enroll me in."

Tilda looked a little guilty. "I didn't mean to hurt your feelings."

I waved my fork around. "You didn't hurt my feelings. It does look ridiculous, but I'd been trying with stones and none of them were successful. I tried the spell on the doll as a joke and when it worked I just got so excited I wanted to show someone. I'll do a proper one at some stage with a very pretty rock. Just let me revel in this one little success for a few minutes."

Tilda waved her hand to grab the attention of the waitress, doing some weird signals that I had no hope of understanding. "You're right. Congratulations are in order. We need cake."

I cocked my head seeing a pattern. "You're having a milkshake and cake for breakfast. What's going on?"

The waitress appeared at our table with two large slabs of chocolate cake. She looked me up and down and sneered. I waited until she left.

"Come on, give. What's going on?"

Tilda took a large piece of cake and shoved it in her mouth. If she thought that was going to stop me questioning her, she was severely underestimating me.

I waited until she finished chewing and pulled her slice away before she could get another one. "Tell me what's going on or you don't get this back."

Tilda narrowed her eyes. "Is this really the hill you want to die on?"

I slid the cake back to her wondering how the situation had escalated so quickly. She reached into her bag and pulled out an envelope.

"What's this?"

"Read it," she said, before shoveling another piece of cake into her mouth.

I opened the envelope and looked at the cream parchment. "It's a wedding invitation."

"Correction, it's a wedding invitation from my ex."

And now everything was made clear. "Why would he send you an invitation to the wedding?"

"Because he wants to rub it in that he has found someone, and I haven't."

"How long ago were you seeing him?"

Tilda frowned as if concentrating. "We broke up four years ago."

"Are you still friends?"

Tilda shook her head. "I haven't seen him since the day we broke up."

That made the situation easier. "Then you just put this in the trash and never think of it again."

"Shouldn't I go? You know, to make him realize that I'm over him."

I snorted. "That is a bad idea. If you go, he will know you aren't over him. Don't go, don't even reply to the invitation, and it will seem like you couldn't care less that he's moved on."

Tilda toyed with her cake. "That sounds like really good advice."

"It's incredible advice," I said as I attacked my own slice of cake. "I've even impressed myself."

Tilda laughed. "You really are in a good mood, aren't you?"

I was about to answer when a movement behind her caught my attention. I watched as the diner door swung open, and my fork fell from my hand. Before I knew what I was doing, I slid so low in my seat I ended up on the floor under the table.

Tilda popped her head down. "What are you doing?"

"Just give me a minute to work something out." I tried to calm my breathing. "I need you to sit up properly and pretend nothing strange is happening."

Tilda did as I said. "Okay, what next?"

"Do you see the guy who just came in? The one who looks like he believes he's God's gift to women?"

Even from under the table I could hear Tilda's sigh. "This is Walker Bay, you just described at least three quarters of the men who live in this town."

"The blond in the green shirt who looks like he spends every available minute in the gym," I said.

There was silence for a few seconds, and I was tempted to put my head up.

"You mean Julian? Myra's brother."

I'm not exaggerating when I say my heart stopped. "Brother?" I croaked.

"Well, technically he's her half-brother. They've got different fathers. He usually travels a lot. I haven't seen him in town for ages." She ducked her head under the table. "He must have only come back in the last day or two, don't tell me you've managed to embarrass yourself in front of him already."

Oh, if she only knew.

"I need you to tell me when he's gone," I said, far more calmly than I felt.

She sat back up again. "Please tell me you're not staying there until he leaves."

Or until the Earth opened up and swallowed me. I was good with either option.

A few minutes later Tilda kicked me. "He's gone."

I peeked over the table. "Are you sure?"

"Of course, I'm sure. Did you want to tell me what that was about?"

"Not particularly."

I settled back in my seat and grabbed my slice of the cake, grateful for Tilda's foresight. If Julian Bernauer was in town, I was going to need it.

2

"*Y*ou know, you're going to have to talk to me sooner or later," Tilda whined.

I was voting for later, like end of the world later, but I knew I had to give her something.

"I know him, and I'd rather not run into him again. Ever."

She followed me out of the diner and stopped me before I could disappear on her. "You must have done something really dumb."

What I'd done had been beyond dumb, and I never wanted to think about it again. I opened my mouth to tell her to leave it be when I heard a voice behind me.

"I knew that was you."

To say I was taken by surprise was an understatement. One second I was trying to avoid a conversation with Tilda, and in the next, I was spun around and swept up into the arms of a man I had believed I would never see again. It took me a couple of moments to realize what was happening, and Julian took advantage of that time to swoop in for a kiss. The second his lips touched mine I snapped out of my shock. I pushed against his chest and was surprised when he flew back. I hadn't thought I was that strong. Everything became clearer when I found him on the ground several feet away with a furious ogre standing over him.

"Buddy, that was all kinds of stupid."

There was no expressing how glad I was to see Deputy Karl Iversen.

"You okay, Sadie?" Karl asked as he kept his eyes on a furious Julian.

I nodded as I stepped back, wanting to put as much distance as I could between me and the man I had been sure was a humiliating memory that I would never have to face again.

"You're going to regret that." Julian pulled himself into a crouch as if preparing to fight. My eyes widened as his hands started to glow. Seems like Julian had been keeping something from me.

Rather than showing any fear, Karl shook his head. "Man, you just assaulted the coven leader's niece in broad daylight. I would suggest you not make matters worse."

Julian gave that charming smile of his. "She's my girlfriend, you idiot. Trust me, that wasn't an assault."

"And the stupid just keeps on going," Karl muttered. "Buddy, I don't know anything about this situation, but there is one thing I can guarantee. You are not involved with this woman in any way, shape or form."

Julian looked up and gave me that heart stopping smile of his. "Tell him, Sadie. Tell him what we have together. Tell him the last thing you said to me."

There were so many things wrong with that statement that I just didn't know where to start. Wait a second, I did know where to start. Staring a stunned Julian in the eye, I wiped my arm across my mouth. "Don't ever come near me again."

Karl smiled approvingly. "I'm pretty sure that says everything that needs to be said." He pointed down the street. "You and I are going to have a little chat. I think you need to be filled in on a few facts of life."

Julian shook his hands and the glowing stopped. He slowly looked me up and down, heat in his eyes. "I'll be seeing you later, babe." He turned and sauntered down the street.

Karl followed him, shaking his head.

"I think there's something you haven't told me."

I turned around to find Tilda with a stunned look on her face.

"There's a few things I haven't told you," I countered.

Tilda swallowed. "Yeah, but this one seems kind of big."

I sighed heavily and wiped my hand across my face. When I looked up, I saw that everyone in the street had stopped to watch the drama unfolding in front of them. "Look, can you give me an hour? I don't want to do this here. And there's somebody else who deserves this explanation first. Come over to my place and I'll tell you everything."

Tilda opened her mouth and I could tell the curiosity was killing her, but I just needed a bit of time. Some of the stress I was feeling must have been showing in my expression because she nodded sharply. "Okay, I'll be at your door in an hour. Do not try leaving before then. I'll just track you down and force you to tell me."

That sounded like a healthy relationship.

I SHOULDN'T HAVE BEEN surprised when I pulled up into my driveway to find the sheriff's truck sitting out the front of my house. Conall met me at the front door and silently waited for me to unlock it. I gestured towards the couch and sat down next to him. Without him saying a word I started what

I was sure was the most uncomfortable conversation of my life.

"I met Julian Bernauer not long after my mother died. I was devastated at losing her and I met him when he was running in the local park." Despite myself I smiled as I remembered. "I was constantly going for walks to clear my head and...well, he must have noticed me. He struck up a conversation with me and, before I knew it, we were seeing each other. I fell hard and fast. And then I told him I loved him, and he disappeared the next day. I tried to contact him, but he'd left his home and none of my calls were returned. At the point I started feeling like a crazy stalker, the job as library assistant in Georgia came up so I took it. Then I got kidnapped by two crazy old ladies and brought here. I had no idea he was paranormal, and I never thought I would see him again. I figured he was just one of those life lessons my mom used to tell me about. She was always trying to warn me about the games men play. I guess after her experience with my father, she was pretty wary about the entire gender." I took in a shaky breath. "That's the whole story. Now that I look back on it, I wonder if I fell so fast because I was desperate to have someone in my life after the only person in the world who loved me was no longer there."

I felt Conall's arm go around my shoulders as the tears started running down my face. I don't know why I was crying. I hated thinking about that time and the utter desolation I had felt. He tugged me closer and I started sobbing in earnest.

It took a while for me to calm down again, and even then I stayed where I was, listening to his heartbeat. It was so strong and solid, and it reminded me that I wasn't alone.

"Do you still have feelings for him?" Conall's voice sounded rough, as if the words were being torn from him.

I pulled myself up and looked at him. There was a vulnerability in those pale blue eyes that captured me every time I looked at them. I wanted to soothe his worries.

"I don't think so."

Conall frowned. "That doesn't sound like a definitive answer."

I wanted to make sure that I explained this to him the right way. "When Julian disappeared, I was devastated. A lot more devastated than I should have been over such a short relationship. To be perfectly honest, we had barely started dating when I thought I'd fallen for him. I think I was just in a weird place emotionally. By the time I was brought here, I'd convinced myself that it was just one of those strange moments in time when you act in a way that is completely contrary to how you always saw yourself. Seeing him today was just not what I ever expected to have happen. I've just been surprised."

Conall looked out the window. "I heard you kissed him."

I pulled back a little bit. "Then your sources are wrong. He barely kissed me when I pushed him away and Karl grabbed him. I was talking to Tilda when he came up behind me." I frowned. "Where is this coming from? I have to deal with your ex-girlfriends everywhere I turn."

Conall lifted his hands up and ran them through his hair. "They were never girlfriends. They were never as important to me as you are. You had real feelings for this guy. There's a difference." He lowered his voice. "I would have chosen you, even without the Destined Beloved prophecy. I'm concerned that you wouldn't have chosen me."

I went to refute him, but he shook his head. "I know this isn't your fault. I just think we need to sort out what you feel. I can't be your second choice and I'm worried that the prophecy is trapping you here." He stood up abruptly. "So, what I'm going to do is give you some space and time to sort out your feelings. I'm here if you want to talk, but other than that I'm not going to bother you."

With that pronouncement, he abruptly turned around and headed for the door, opening it to find a bewildered Tilda. He tipped his hat and got past her before I could call him back.

"That looks like it went well," Tilda drawled.

3

"*I*t hasn't been an hour," I said dryly.

Tilda pushed her way in. "You didn't really think I'd wait that long, did you?"

"I hoped." I went to the kitchen to grab some water. After the amount of sobbing I'd done on Conall's shirt I had a feeling I was dehydrated.

"Is he right?" Tilda asked. "Would you have chosen him without the prophecy.

"I don't know," I said honestly. "I know I was attracted to him, but with his reputation I would probably have given him a wide berth." I sighed as memories rushed towards me. "I got my heart ripped apart by a bad boy not too long ago. I can't say that I would have been keen to repeat the experience."

"That's not good. Conall Tolan is not the sort of man who could handle being second best."

I shook my head. "He is not second best. He would never be second best. He is the most amazing man I have ever known. He is strong, kind, understanding..."

"Rude, surly, controlling." Tilda completed.

"He's still a good man," I countered.

"I'm not arguing that." I could see Tilda was trying to make a point, but for the life of me I couldn't see what it was.

"Look at it from his point of view," Tilda said patiently. "All his life he's had shallow relationships that meant absolutely nothing. Now he's dealing with a Destined Beloved prophecy. That's like going from counting using your toes to a Nobel prize for math in the blink of an eye. He's got to be feeling overwhelmed. You guys have finally decided not to fight the prophecy and to actually start…," she waved her hand around, "whatever it is that you guys are doing, and all of a sudden some guy you actually cared about has turned up. No wonder he's panicking."

"I don't want him to panic," I said glumly. "I like him. I don't want him upset."

Tilda rolled her eyes. "That's a passionate response.

"This situation is new to me," I snapped. "I'm doing the best I can here."

We both looked up at the loud knock on the door.

"I can't deal with this," I muttered as I opened the door to find a ticked off Seer. "What are you doing here, Agnes?"

Agnes swept past me and threw herself down on the couch next to Tilda. "I heard you were making out with Julian Bernauer on the main street of town, in front of everyone, when you are subject to my one and only Destined Beloved prophecy. I'm here to make sure that isn't true."

"It's not true," I was starting to feel really tired.

She looked at me expectantly.

"He kissed me. I pushed him away and then Karl grabbed him. There was barely a second worth of lip contact."

"Sometimes that's all it takes," she said, in a way that sounded like she had the wisdom of the world at her fingertips.

I frowned. "Why is everyone so invested in this? You've

all been telling me that a Destined Beloved prophecy couldn't be broken. This situation shouldn't even matter."

Agnes sighed as if she was having to explain something to an idiot. "A Destined Beloved prophecy means you are soul mates, linked for all eternity. It doesn't stop you from doing something stupid. You're still human. More or less."

My answer to that was interrupted by the door flying open and an angry ogre storming into my house. It was a sign of how much my life had changed that I wasn't the least bit disturbed by this latest turn of events.

"Do you want to explain to me what just happened," Karl growled.

"Didn't you just go off with him?" I queried. "I thought you would talk to him."

Seeing as Tilda and Agnes had taken up residence on the couch, Karl grabbed a chair and swung his leg over. "He wasn't going to tell me squat. Just said that his day was looking up and then asked me where you were living."

"You didn't tell him, did you?" I asked as I started wondering if I needed to get Flora to put up some stronger wards around the house. The current ones turned any intruders who were not welcome into my house into giant crystal statues. Not very subtle, but I'd seen first-hand how effective it was."

Karl gave me a sour look. "Of course, I didn't tell him. But he'll work it out sooner or later. I need to know what you're going to do when he does find you."

"I have no idea," I replied. "I didn't even know Julian was a witch." I stopped to think about what I'd seen him do. "He is a witch, right? There isn't something else that does weird glowing hands?"

"Definitely a witch," Tilda replied. "His father is a member of the Conclave. Comes from a very powerful witch family. Rumor has it Myra's mother wanted a daughter from that bloodline. She stalked him and got him drunk. Very drunk. Next thing you know, she's pregnant and he's furious. When it ended up being a boy she wasn't as interested. Word is she accepted a lot of money to give the father custody. When he became an adult, he came back to meet his mother and sister, but there's really not much of a relationship there."

"In the version I got, his dad was a banker and his mom was some stripper who got knocked up."

Tilda snorted. "That's funny. I'm never going to be able to look at Violet Hallybread without thinking about that now." Tilda frowned as if she was remembering something. "Did you know that he was engaged?"

I got a sick feeling in my stomach. "Please tell me he just got engaged after a whirlwind romance."

Tilda shook her head. "They've been engaged forever. Both have family members who are a part of the Conclave. Family bloodlines that go back forever. They're like witch royalty."

"He was engaged." I could hear my voice rising and there it was. Confusion had taken a backseat to overwhelming anger. That jerk made me the other woman. Next time I was going to kick him where it hurt.

"This is all very interesting," Karl interrupted sarcastically. "But I don't think you're realizing how much this mess is going to affect my life."

"When did this situation become all about you?" I asked.

"When I have to work every day with the man who is going to make my life a living hell until you convince him that he is your one and only."

"I don't even know whether he is."

"He's your Destined Beloved!" Agnes shouted, surprising everyone. "Of course, he is."

I was going to have to remember she didn't deal well when questioned. I pointed at her. "You know, that kind of attitude is why we're in the mess we're in. Why can't everybody just forget about the prophecy and let us work this out like two normal people."

"Because normal people don't get a Destined Beloved prophecy," Tilda said quietly. "Only extraordinary ones do. It's a momentous event brought about by fate."

"And that's the problem," I said. "When emotions come into it, things get messy, even when fate is involved." I looked around at the group of people who seemed to be almost as invested in my romantic life as I was. "I think you need to let us work this out ourselves."

I could see this was not the most welcome suggestion I could have given them. Fortunately, any argument they might have offered was intercepted by Tilda's and my phones going off at the same time. Tilda grabbed hers. "There's a meeting of both covens. Everyone has to be there."

I checked my phone and found the same message.

"Both covens," Agnes repeated. "That can't be good."

Karl stood up and started heading for the door. "I'll warn the sheriff. If both covens are working together it probably means we're facing an apocalypse. We need to be ready."

"That's a cynical way of looking at it," I noted.

"Probably accurate, though," replied Tilda. "We'd better get going. I'm sure my grandmother has a heap of jobs she wants me to do before the meeting."

"I'll go with you. I need to talk to Flora before she finds out about Julian and starts freaking out like everybody else in this town seems to be." I went to grab my purse when I was stopped by Agnes.

"I'm coming too."

"No, you're not." Tilda seemed indignant at Agnes's statement.

"Why can't she come?" I asked, curious at the way Tilda

and Agnes seemed to be shaping up to each other. "The meeting is for all witches."

"Except the Seer," Tilda replied through gritted teeth. "The Seer is to remain separate from the covens to ensure complete impartiality of her visions."

"I'm going," Agnes said flatly. "I want to know what's going on. Either you take me with you or I sneak in myself, and who knows what kind of trouble I could get myself into."

She didn't sound like she was going to take no for an answer. I glanced at Tilda and found her glaring at me as if this was all my fault.

"Fine, we'll take you, but you need to be discreet."

Agnes jumped up and grabbed me for a hug. "Thank you so much."

I avoided Tilda's death stare. I don't know what she was worried about. If this went sideways, I was going to be the one blamed.

4

*D*ue to the fact we were now sneaking the Seer in, it was decided that it would be better for Tilda to go ahead of us and offer to help with the organization of the meeting. Agnes and I would come in about ten minutes before the meeting started when everybody else would turn up. Hopefully, we would be lost in the sea of faces. Guessing that our luck wouldn't hold that well, we did our best to make Agnes look a little less conspicuous. Her black clothes were replaced with color and patterns and her spiky black hair was covered with a blonde wig that Tilda had laying around. There were going to be questions about that at a later time, but for now we had other priorities.

"How do I look?" Agnes asked nervously as she brushed her hands down her shirt once we'd parked out the front of the meeting hall.

I looked at her critically. "You look like everybody."

"That's not a compliment."

I opened the car door. "I'm all out of compliments today. You should have insisted Tilda stay with you if you wanted an ego boost."

We fell in behind another group who had just arrived and made our way to the back of the room. At least this time the sheriff wasn't invited to the meeting, so I didn't have to worry about the inbuilt sensor he seemed to have when it came to finding me.

"Keep your head down," I muttered as I kept an eye out for anyone who could identify the Seer.

It took a while for people to take their seats and quiet to descend on the room. Flora headed to the stage at the front of the hall, Violet Hallybread following her. Violet's graying hair was intricately bound in a scarf and her full-length dress swayed with each step. Behind her came the other two leaders of the Path Coven. Elspeth Pickering drew attention with a fuchsia colored dress that almost hurt the eyes. Ilsa Hocking was striking in stark black. Her daughter, Jeanette, had been brutally murdered by the same man who had kidnapped me. Word was that she would never recover from the pain of losing her only child. Seeing the way she looked now forced me to agree with that assessment.

I noticed Violet's daughter, Myra, sitting at the front of the hall, her face sporting a scowl. Now that I looked at the way people were seated, I could see that it was almost like a wedding. The Walker Bay Coven on one side of the hall, a bustling group of men and women. On the other side was the Path Coven, a smaller group that consisted of just women. For some reason, all males born into the Path Coven were tossed out when they reached the age of fourteen. The Walker Bay Coven took in these boys until they were adults and gave them the choice to either join the coven or walk away. I couldn't understand that mentality, but the Path Coven had the belief that males in the coven weakened them somehow. Even though there were seats available on the Path side, I could see that witches from the Walker Bay Coven preferred to stand around the edges. On their side of course.

"They don't look too friendly with each other, do they?" I muttered to Agnes.

Agnes looked around and frowned when she noticed the same division as I did. "This is all so childish. It drives me crazy."

"Keep your voice down," I hissed as I realized people were starting to notice her rising tone.

As Flora and Violet took to the stage, the noise in the hall died down. Violet stepped back and let Flora take the lead, although her body language clearly indicated that she was only doing it under duress.

Flora's voice rang clear through the hall. "As most of you know there was a recent incident in Walker Bay where a trusted member of our community started dabbling in the dark arts."

There was a rumbling in the crowd. Everyone knew that Flora had been the victim of Isobel's curse.

"As a result, the Conclave has sent a team of magisters to investigate Isobel and ensure the corruption has been contained by her confinement."

My heart sank at the announcement that the magister had finally arrived in Walker Bay. Flora had been warning me that the Conclave was going to investigate the Isobel situation, but the longer time passed, the more I hoped that Walker Bay would be left alone. It looked like our period of grace was coming to a screeching end.

Flora gestured to the front row. "I wish to welcome Magister Julian Bernauer, Magister Penelope Hartford and Magister Liam Rigby to Walker Bay. May your efforts bring peace and comfort to our community."

Agnes elbowed me in the side and I barely felt it. My eyes tracked the three magisters as they headed up to the stage where Flora stood, looking far more serene than I would have thought possible under these circumstances. Violet smiled, her feelings about having the magister being her son, obvious to everyone.

"This cannot be good," whispered Agnes, and I appreciated her understatement. The one man who I was desperate to avoid, was also the one man who could destroy my life, or end it.

As I watched the stage, I could see my aunt's eyes on me, her concern almost palpable. I drew in a shaky breath, hoping that the fear I was feeling was not obvious to everyone else.

Julian stood at the front of the stage, his eyes sweeping the entire room. Every time they went past me I fought the inclination to drop my head, sure that the sudden movement would draw his attention. That was the very last thing I wanted.

"As Coven Leader Harstone has said, we are here to investigate the dark magic used in Walker Bay. Our intention is to protect our citizens here, not to lay blame." Julian's smooth voice rumbled out over the hall, and I'm sure it would be comforting if I didn't know without a doubt that his job was to find people like me and turn them over to the Conclave.

"We will be interviewing everybody individually. Please make yourself available as there will be no exceptions."

And there went my fleeting thought that right about now would be a perfect time for a holiday, anywhere but here. Julian's words were polite, but the tone was commanding.

Violet stepped forward and put her hand on Julian's arm, her claiming of her son an obvious power play. "The Path Coven welcomes the magisters to Walker Bay. We will cooperate fully."

Flora inclined her head, seemingly reluctant to indulge Violet's need for a theatrical statement.

"Thank you, Magister Bernauer." Flora turned to the

two covens. "The last couple of months has seen our community go through unimaginable pain. Both covens have lost members. Isobel to dark magic, and Jeanette and Jaxon to violence. It is at these times when we should pull together."

Her eyes alighted on me and I could see a slight frown cross her face. "After all, we are family, and nothing is more important than family."

I caught the meaning in her words and felt tears sting the back of my eyes. It had been a while since I had felt that I belonged anywhere. Flora had given me a home, and more importantly, she was trying to give me the family I so desperately craved.

When the meeting broke up I watched as the two groups kept glancing furtively at each other. Despite Flora's fervent wish that the community would come together, I didn't see that happening. Perhaps the breach between the two covens was too much for them to ever unite. I hoped not. If there was really somebody targeting Walker Bay that was as powerful as I feared they were, we were going to need to work together.

I smiled as I could see Tilda trying to be nonchalant as she made her way towards us. "Your aunt wants to talk to you," she hissed. "She's not happy that you came so late."

She'd be even less happy if she knew the reason why I was late. "Can you stay here and look after you know who while I talk to her."

"On it," Tilda replied with all the seriousness of a secret service agent.

"You know, I'm right here and I'm perfectly capable of looking after myself." Agnes sounded a little miffed at our actions, but considering how much trouble we could be in for smuggling her into this meeting, I wasn't going to indulge her.

"Stay here," I ordered, figuring she couldn't get much more annoyed than she already was.

I made my way over to Flora and waited patiently while she finished talking to some of the coven members who needed a bit more hand holding than the others. Once they were dismissed, she stepped over to me and pulled me into a hug.

"I hear today was a little trying for you," she murmured against my ear.

"How much do you know?"

"Just that you were making out with a magister in the main street. Not precisely the way I would have suggested you deal with this situation, but inventive and to the point if nothing else."

I rolled my eyes and decided to give her the cliff notes version. "I started seeing him after my mom died. He bolted the day after I told him I loved him. He's the reason I think men suck. He kissed me, not the other way around. Now Conall's giving me space and every one of my friends is telling me how this situation affects them."

Flora stepped back and tucked some of my hair behind my ear. "I support whatever you decide. I will counsel you to be careful." Those words were loaded with meaning. "You may want to keep your distance from the magister in anything other than a professional setting. I believe his fiancée was a little upset by today's display."

My heart sank. "She's the other magister, isn't she?" My mind cast back to the delicate woman I had seen on stage.

"She is," Flora confirmed. "After today, I think you will definitely be on her radar."

I groaned and dropped my head. Maybe I should go on a road trip, far away from witches and werewolves and ex-boyfriends with fiancées.

"Now, please get the Seer out of here before anyone else

spots her." Flora smiled sweetly at me, but there was no escaping the command in her tone.

"I will," I said meekly.

I turned around to find Julian's eyes on me. For a moment we were locked together as if we were the only two people in the world. He went to step towards me but was stopped by his sister as she insistently pulled on his arm. I had never been more grateful to Myra Hallybread than I was in that moment. I quickly made my way to Tilda and had to stop myself from laughing at the way she was trying to discreetly shield Agnes from the rest of the room.

"We need to get you out of here now."

Tilda groaned. "She knows, doesn't she?"

Agnes snorted. "Of course, she knows. There's a reason she was chosen to be the coven leader at the age of thirteen."

As we hustled a protesting Agnes out the door, I felt eyes on me. I resisted the overwhelming temptation to look back, knowing that whatever I saw was going to complicate my life in ways I wasn't ready to handle.

5

*A*fter a restless night I'd decided I didn't have the strength or the answers to deal with my well-meaning friends, so I had avoided my usual breakfast at the diner and gone straight to work. In the few weeks that I had been living in Walker Bay I had come to see the library as a sort of sanctuary. The knowledge I was accumulating about the world I had found myself in was invaluable. Despite the coven's resistance to technology, I had started cataloguing the books on my own laptop. One day I was hoping the coven would see the value in not having to spend hours combing through ancient texts looking for a particular spell. Although, as Tilda told me, some of the witches enjoyed the process, no matter how long it took them. Unfortunately, at times I found myself distracted by the fascinating information I was discovering. The books didn't just contain spells, they provided a window into a time and culture that was completely alien to me.

As I was working on a book from the seventeenth century the sound of a text coming through on my phone seemed ridiculously incongruous. My heart dropped when I discovered that my interview with the magisters was scheduled for the following day. It was too soon. I wasn't ready to face my greatest fear. I fumbled with my phone, wanting to call Flora and be reassured that everything was going to be alright.

"So, this is where you've been hiding."

I looked up at the sound of the last voice I wanted to hear.

"How did you get in?" I gasped as I dropped my phone on the table. "There are wards around this building. I have to give specific entrance to everybody at the moment."

Those security processes had been put in place after I was kidnapped from the library.

Julian wiggled his fingers. "Magister, remember. There aren't many things I can't do."

Considering my secret, that was a pretty horrifying thought.

"My interview is tomorrow." I couldn't stop myself from talking. I grabbed my phone and held it up to show him. "Tomorrow afternoon, not today."

Julian smiled, his brown eyes sparking with amusement. He always used to say that I made him laugh. I wanted to bang my head against the desk. This was not the time to remember things like that.

"The rest of my team is doing the interviews with my mother and sister this morning. Need to ensure there is no chance of bias." He sat down in the chair opposite me, his demeanor deceptively calm. "I was surprised to find you here."

"No more than I was to see you," I countered.

"You never told me you were a witch."

"Neither did you."

Julian ran his hand through his blond hair. "My understanding was that you'd been brought up in the normal world. I had no inkling you were a witch, much less from a coven leader's family."

His words sounded casual, but I wasn't fooled. He wanted information. I inwardly steeled myself. I could do this.

"It seems my father was a witch. My understanding is he was Flora's nephew." I laughed nervously. "According to Flora I'm family and she doesn't seem to need a DNA test, so we're going with that for now."

"You weren't raised by a witch," Julian mused. "Strange that you knew about that side of you."

"My mother told me about the paranormal world," I said hurriedly, silently apologizing to the woman who taught me it was never acceptable to lie. "I'm not sure how she knew about it."

I was quickly learning that there were some circumstances where lying was an absolute must. For example, if I told Julian the truth, that I knew nothing about the paranormal world until the day that I was kidnapped and dragged here against my will, then two sweet, although slightly deranged, little old ladies could find themselves in a world of trouble. Seeing as one of those ladies was Tilda's grandmother, I was willing to lie my butt off to protect her. I was sure my mother would be okay with that.

"I'm sorry I left when I did." Julian leaned back. "My job sometimes calls me away at inconvenient times."

"That doesn't explain not answering any of my messages or phone calls," I bit out, embarrassment streaking through me. I know that over those few days after he'd left I'd gone overboard with trying to contact him, but I'd been so hurt and couldn't believe that he would ghost me like that.

Julian grimaced. "You know the rules. We can play with normals, we just can't get serious with them."

Wow, that hurt more than I expected it to. I'd been all in with the relationship with Julian, no matter how short it had been. I did not need this right now. "I was surprised." I hoped I sounded casual and didn't give away any of the searing pain I had felt at his desertion. "I was even more surprised when I found out you had a fiancée when we were seeing each other."

He waved his hand in the air. "A minor detail, one of those arranged things."

"Well, some things are best left in the past."

"Six months ago, I would have said the same thing," he said and gave me that charming smile of his. "But now everything's changed."

"It has," I agreed, not returning his smile. "I'm not sure if you've heard, but I'm the subject of a Destined Beloved prophecy."

"I've heard," he said.

"With a berserker werewolf." I expected that to at least give him pause. I had watched a man literally run away from me when he found out who I was. And I meant literally in the precise definition of the term.

"Myra filled me in."

Of course, she had. Despite us having an alliance of sorts several weeks ago, I could still count on Myra's anger at Conall dumping her when they were in high school.

"My understanding is that we are soul mates, destined to be together forever."

Julian inclined his head. "That's one interpretation."

As far as I knew that was the only interpretation. "What are you talking about?"

"Some academics believe the Destined Beloved prophecy was misnamed. It was more about two beings of power coming together in a symbiotic relationship rather than a romantic one. In fact, some theorize that it would be better to leave the emotional part out of the prophecy."

I stared at him, stunned and disbelieving.

"Those academics are wrong," growled my Destined Beloved from the doorway.

I glanced up, and for the first time today I smiled.

"If there are wards here, how did he get in?" Julian asked, the curiosity in his eyes obvious.

Conall smiled in a way that made me think of a shark. "I can get into any place where Sadie is. Seems to be a side effect of the Destined Beloved prophecy.

That, and an unerring sense of direction when it came to me. I still didn't know how I felt about that.

Conall turned to me, effectively dismissing Julian. "I came to pick you up for lunch."

Despite his high-handed tone, I refused to argue with him in front of Julian.

"Great, let's get going." I glared pointedly at Julian, and for a change he got the message.

"I'll see you tomorrow at your interview."

I frowned. "Shouldn't Magister Rigby be interviewing me? You know, to ensure there is no accusation of bias."

Julian gave another smile. "Normally yes, but I'm the senior magister. I make the rules."

Conall stood next to me and deliberately put an arm around my waist in a move that wasn't even close to being subtle.

Julian grinned at the obvious power play and headed out. He turned as he opened the door. "Despite the rules of our world, I couldn't keep away. I came back for you, but you'd already left. I've been looking for you ever since."

With that bombshell he walked out, leaving me with a seething berserker.

"How upset would you be if I tore him apart," Conall asked, his voice deceptively calm.

"At the moment, not all that upset." I had a thought. "Don't challenge him, he's supposed to be pretty powerful.

Conall gave me a look that spoke volumes about what he thought of my warning.

"Don't glare at me like that. I, better than anyone, know how strong you are, but there is always going to be something or someone that is stronger. It's the way of the world, and I prefer to keep you in one piece."

"That's good to know," he murmured, looking down at me with heat in his eyes. He dropped his head and slowly explored my lips. This wasn't the passionate claiming we'd had before but it was no less devastating.

When we finally broke apart, I felt bereft. "What was that?" I gasped, still trying to get my breath back.

"I couldn't sleep last night thinking about you. According to my deputies I'm too cranky to be allowed around the public today. All because of you. Bernauer is wrong. What's between us is all about the emotion. I'm not giving that up without a fight."

I leaned my head against his chest and felt his heartbeat. I would never tell him how much his walking away yesterday had hurt me. Or how much his willingness to fight for us soothed that hurt.

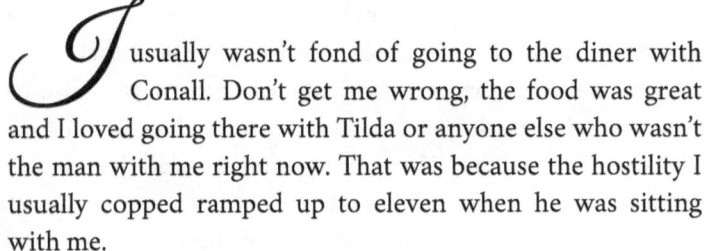

6

I usually wasn't fond of going to the diner with Conall. Don't get me wrong, the food was great and I loved going there with Tilda or anyone else who wasn't the man with me right now. That was because the hostility I usually copped ramped up to eleven when he was sitting with me.

"Have you got that troll doll thing of yours?"

"Sure," I said as I pulled it out of my bag. "Why?"

"I'd rather today we have a private conversation that nobody could overhear."

I grinned and activated the doll. I was still ridiculously proud of what I'd done. There is nothing like your first successful spell. There were times when I thought that I would never get there, and that the only magical thing about me was my cursebreaking ability. An ability that carried a death sentence in this world. It was a sobering thought, especially as the person who was most dangerous to me was Julian.

After we put our orders in and I'd watched the requisite

simpering over Conall by the waitress, I leaned back in my seat.

"You seem to have changed your attitude from yesterday."

A slash of red colored Conall's face. "It was brought to my attention that my actions yesterday may have had more to do with my pride than with any real wish to give you space to make a decision." He sighed and ran a hand over his face. "If I'm being completely honest, I was jealous. I know that this world and this prophecy have been thrust on you. It's not ideal. And then there's Bernauer. You were in love with him before everything changed for you, and he's a witch. In an ideal world he would be perfect for you. Or at least a much better option for you than a berserker werewolf. All I could see was that the only thing holding us together was the prophecy, and you've never been very happy about that.

I tried to organize my thoughts. I knew my response to what he said was important to our future. "Yes, I did love him, but I'm not sure how much of that was due to the emotion of that time. I did want to fight the prophecy, but I know there's something between us and there's no changing that, despite what Julian said."

Our orders arrived and we started eating.

"What did you think about what he said about two beings of power?" Conall asked.

I pointed to the troll doll. "I think it's obvious."

He threw back his head and laughed.

"I knew that you were the only person who could put him in a good mood."

I looked up into the twinkling gray eyes of a much happier ogre.

"It looks like you found a way to fix your problem, Deputy Iversen." I had no doubt that it was Karl who had convinced Conall to look beyond his pride.

Karl sat in the booth next to me and snagged some fries

from my plate. "You have no idea how grumpy this man was this morning."

"Deputy…" Conall growled, the warning clear in his tone.

Karl completely ignored him. "We were about to have a mutiny in the office."

"Oh, this is good, I was beginning to get worried."

Tilda slid into the booth next to the sheriff and waved her hand between me and Conall. "How did this happen?"

"Well…"

"I had a talk to the sheriff about how pride and stupidity don't mix well with stable relationships," Karl interrupted my explanation.

I was surprised. The deputy was usually the calm one in the group.

"I'd like to state for the record that I would have got there on my own eventually," Conall pointed out.

"Not soon enough," grumbled Karl, which more than anything showed how unpleasant his morning had been.

The diner door opened, and the three magisters walked in.

Conall followed my gaze and growled. "I should have known he'd try something."

Tilda glanced over at me. "At least you're not hiding under the table this time," she quipped.

I shrugged helplessly as Conall's and Karl's heads swung in my direction. "I didn't handle the surprise well yesterday. Sue me." I watched as Julian and his team headed in our direction, the look on Julian's face indicating he was ready for a confrontation. "Be nice," I murmured.

"You don't know us at all if you're expecting nice," whispered Tilda.

I couldn't help it. I giggled. "I can't believe you're all so keen to protect my virtue."

"Sure," Karl drawled. "Keep thinking that's what we're doing."

"Sadie," Julian said as he stood next to our table. "Would you like to introduce me to your friends?"

Not particularly, but I didn't see a way out of it. "Magister Bernauer, you already know Sheriff Tolan. This is Deputy Iversen and Tilda Atwill. All good friends of mine. All willing to hurt you if you get too close to me." I smiled sweetly.

Julian chuckled. "Good to know." He turned to the rest of his team. "This is Liam Rigby and Penelope Hartford. We will be conducting interviews with both covens, sometimes separately, sometimes together."

"I'm a little surprised that you haven't seen fit to inform the sheriff's office about this investigation." Conall looked relaxed despite the serious conversation.

I cringed when Julian adopted a condescending tone that was sure to annoy Conall. "This is Conclave business. It has nothing to do with the sheriff."

Conall lifted an eyebrow. "I'm sure that's what the magister who was investigating the Palmerston incident thought. Things didn't end too well for him, did they?"

For the first time since I'd met him, Julian looked agitated. "How do you know about that? Nobody is supposed to know about that."

Conall gave the smile of a man who knows he's won a skirmish. "You'd be shocked at what I know."

Julian gave a tight nod and stalked away, the other two magisters close behind. As they left I didn't miss the daggers from Magister Hartford. It seemed I had managed to make another enemy without even trying. I was beginning to think it was a gift.

"Man, he's hot," Tilda sighed.

All three of us glared at her.

"I meant Rigby," she protested.

"So, what happened at Palmerston?" I asked.

Conall grimaced. "I can't really say anything about what happened. It's just good for the magisters that visit this town to know that, despite what they believe, their power is not unlimited." He glanced at Karl. "It's time for us to get back to work."

Karl grabbed a couple more of my fries and stood up. Tilda let Conall out the booth, and then promptly sat back down again.

Conall came over and kissed me sweetly, his thumb caressing my cheek. "I'll see you tonight," he whispered, before leaving with his deputy.

Tilda grinned. "That looked like things are back on an even keel."

"It does, doesn't it?"

Tilda looked serious all of a sudden. "Are you happy?" she asked. "A lot has happened to you in the last couple of months and you've seemed to weather it so well that we really haven't checked with you.

I looked out through the diner window and, as I watched the sexy sheriff explain to a belligerent centaur that he did not in fact have right of way, I smiled. "Yeah, I'm happy."

7

This time I made sure to lock the library door before starting on my work. There was no way I wanted any more surprises. I'd barely started when the door opened. Sometimes I wondered why I even bothered doing normal things like locking doors. In a paranormal town there was always somebody who could get through them. At least this time I had some warning.

"We need to talk."

It wasn't often that Flora pulled the coven leader card, but I had a feeling that today was not the day to argue. "Where?"

"Where we won't be overheard."

Inwardly I groaned. Flora had a favorite spot where she was sure that no matter how powerful another witch was, they wouldn't be able to overhear us. Unfortunately, this spot was at the top of a hill and required a pretty vigorous hike that I was not yet fit enough for.

A couple of hours later I crashed to the ground and watched Flora create a magic circle for us to sit in so we could have this conversation. When I say sit I meant she was going to sit because I was never going to move again.

"I was interviewed by the magister this morning," she started quite calmly.

If I'd had any energy left in me at all I would have straightened up at that statement.

"How did it go?" I asked.

Flora grimaced. "How does a meeting with representatives of the Conclave ever go?"

From her expression I was assuming not well.

"I do need you to tell me about your relationship with Magister Bernauer."

"Why?" I asked.

"I think it might be important for me to understand where he is coming from."

Though it was the last thing I wanted to do, I told my aunt all about my time with Julian. With her calm manner and gentle questions she was able to tease out of me more information than I had given anyone.

"Sounds like it was a pretty intense time for you," she said thoughtfully. "Do you trust him?"

I shrugged. "Before he left I would have said yes. I had no reason to doubt him. After he completely cut contact with me, I would say no. Especially since now I know he was hiding a couple of huge secrets from me, including a fiancée."

Flora snorted. "I wouldn't put much stock in that relationship. Members of the Conclave have a habit of organizing marriages for their offspring, and ambition means their children follow those plans. Everybody's trying to breed a stronger witch."

"That sounds lovely." It was amazing to me that this could happen, even in the paranormal world.

Flora looked out over what was admittedly a gorgeous view. "How does this change your feelings for the sheriff?"

"It doesn't. I'll just have to deal with Julian the best way I can and keep him away from Conall."

She tucked a strand of hair behind my ear. "Your interview is tomorrow."

And now we got to what was giving her that strained look.

"You're worried about me," I concluded.

"The magisters were the ones who rounded up the curse-breakers for their executions many years ago," she said. "As far as you're concerned, Julian Bernauer is the most dangerous man alive. The reason I'm worried is because his prior relationship with you gives him leverage that he will use to find out the truth."

"What truth?" I tried to give my aunt an encouraging smile. "I was the one left behind while the rest of the coven worked on breaking the curse. Then, when Isobel tried to cast a new curse it backfired on her. Now she's trapped and can't dispute that account." A thought hit me. "She is trapped, isn't she? He can't find a way to talk to her, can he?"

"I hope not," Flora whispered fervently.

That did not sound encouraging. "What did he ask you?"

I was surprised when Flora laid down next to me, her hand holding mine. "He started by asking me what happened and how the curse worked. I told him about being trapped and how I was able to communicate to the rest of the coven through our relationship." She turned her head to me. "He then started asking about you. How you came to arrive in Walker Bay and what has happened since. He's also very interested in the Destined Beloved prophecy."

"Everybody's interested in the Destined Beloved prophecy. It seems to be the most interesting thing about me."

"Only the most interesting thing everybody knows about." Flora corrected. I could feel her grip on my hand becoming tighter as if she was frightened that I would be torn away from her.

"He makes me nervous," she admitted. "It's bad enough that we have magisters in town, but he seems to have an intense interest in you. I can see it causing problems."

I stared at the clouds in the sky. "If he pushes too hard Conall is going to go all berserker on him. He won't be a problem after that."

"That's not an ideal outcome," Flora said dryly.

I didn't think it would be.

"Tarquin is going to be in the interview with you tomorrow."

A part of me liked the idea of having a lawyer with me who was also a vampire. There was also a part of me that was concerned. "Doesn't that scream that I have something to hide?"

Flora shook her head. "I'm having an advocate present for all interviews. Either Tarquin or one of his partners. I won't let my people be railroaded into admitting to something that isn't true." Her voice vibrated with a protective rage.

"I understand why the Seer chose you as the coven leader. You care more about your people than power. That's what makes you the best choice.

Flora smiled at me wistfully. "Isobel never understood that. Going after more power makes you a target. The people in this coven are happy. They have good lives and they have the opportunity to cherish their families. You stick your head up in witch politics and it is liable to get shot off. That's what I am trying to protect us from." Flora sighed. "Maybe I chose the wrong path for us. Maybe if we were considered stronger, we wouldn't have to worry about the Conclave and magisters."

I looked over at the woman who was patiently trying to teach me about being a witch, despite my seeming ineptness. I squeezed her hand and laid my head against her shoulder.

41

"This is what's important," I murmured. "Not power, not making people fear you."

By the time we got back to the library, darkness was beginning to fall. I gave my aunt a hug and set off home. I'd tried to be upbeat with Flora, but the fact of the matter was that I was worried about the upcoming interview with Julian. The Julian I knew was flirty and funny. I didn't know Magister Bernauer, and Flora was right. He knew me quite well. I was afraid that would give him an advantage.

I couldn't help the smile that crossed my face when I saw the sheriff's truck sitting out the front of my house. I pulled up next to it and frowned when I couldn't see him in the front seat. I stepped out of my car only to hear the banging of a hammer. Following the noise, I climbed up the rickety outside steps at the side of the house that led to the deck that sat on top of the garage.

"What are you doing?" I called out after I'd enjoyed the sight of his muscles flexing while hammering away at the floor.

Conall stopped hammering and looked over at me. "Please tell me you didn't come up those steps."

"Of course not. I flew. Flora decided after the troll doll cone of silence spell I was an accomplished enough spell caster to learn how to defy the laws of both nature and physics."

I know he was trying to look stern, but I could see the way his lips quirked upwards. "You know, sarcasm is not your most attractive trait."

"Trust me, it isn't the worst one I have either."

"This place is a death trap. I can't believe Flora's letting her own niece live here."

I carefully made my way over to him, skirting around the edge of the deck which I had learned from painful experience was the most secure area. "Flora believes that family shouldn't interfere with business."

He grasped my hand when I reached him and pulled me against his body. "I know you haven't been walking to the park like you used to ever since…" He trailed off and tightened his grip around me.

He knew that I had been too scared to go on my early morning walks ever since his brother had murdered another witch at my favorite spot. He had then kidnapped me and threatened to tear me apart and leave the pieces of my body there for Conall to find. I still had nightmares. Conall had taken to sharing my bed to hold me and rock me back to sleep when I woke up, terrified that I hadn't got away from Brian. Our relationship hadn't yet taken any further steps, but I relished the safety I found in his arms.

He ran his hand down my back. "This deck has a great view and I thought that if it was safe you could come out here and it would be almost as good." His voice trailed off.

Ever since I'd moved into this house I had regularly come home from work and found Conall fixing one thing or the other. I hadn't been blowing smoke when I told Tilda that he was the best man I had ever known. I tightened my arms around him.

"Thank you," I breathed. "That was really sweet of you."

"I brought some Chinese over for dinner. It might need heating up, but I figured the last thing we would want to do tonight is cook."

I nodded against his chest, reluctant to move. We stayed there for a few minutes, bathed in the moonlight, just enjoying the feel of being in each other's arms. The peace was interrupted when my stomach rumbled and Conall choked off a laugh.

"Let's get you fed."

We organized the food into bowls and sat down on the couch.

"Did you want to tell me where you've been all afternoon?" Conall asked lightly.

"Couldn't you tell?" I countered.

We had recently discovered that Conall had a way of finding me no matter where I was. It was like I had a locator chip embedded in me that only he had access to. It was both a disturbing and comforting situation.

Conall grimaced. "I try not to use it unless there's a good reason."

"I was out with Flora. We went on that hike she loves to take me on."

"Why would she do that? I would have thought she'd be too busy with the magisters in town."

My life depended on my never telling anybody about my cursebreaker ability. That was becoming more and more difficult the more I became embedded in other people's lives. Especially when it came to Conall.

"She wanted to talk, and she felt too constricted in town." I know I was being deliberately vague, but I wasn't yet ready to out myself as a cursebreaker to anybody. It wasn't that I didn't trust Conall. I trusted him more than anyone. Twice he had rescued me from a horrific fate. I just wasn't ready to share my secret with anybody.

"Anything exciting happen at the sheriff's department?"

Conall pushed his food away. "There's something I need to talk to you about."

It didn't take a genius to know that whatever came out of his mouth next was not going to be something I was happy with. I could see that he was looking for the best way to tell me something unpleasant.

"Brigitte Hanlon has been assigned to the department as a liaison from the state police."

My fork dropped with a clatter to the plate. "You're kidding me."

Conall wiped his hand across his face. "I wish I was. Trust me, I don't want it, but I can't get rid of her until she does something actionable."

"You mean, totally messing up a murder investigation and corrupting all the forensic evidence wasn't enough to get her fired, if not jailed."

Conall jumped to his feet and started pacing. "You think I want somebody that toxic in my department? I don't, but the state police can embed an officer in any town, and we have to have a really good reason to refuse."

"How long?" I asked quietly.

Conall shrugged helplessly. "As long as they feel they need her here."

"Any chance your father is behind this?"

"Every chance." Conall sighed and I could see his frustration. "We're going to need to be careful of every piece of information. She's there to do my father's bidding."

I leaned back against the couch and closed my eyes. Detective Brigitte Hanlon was going to be a problem. She was completely under the werewolf alpha's control and she wanted Conall. Those two things were going to be a disaster in his office. Conall dropped down next to me.

"Anything else happen today?" I asked as I leaned my head against his chest.

"Not really," Conall replied as he stroked my hair away from my face. "A patrol found a body out by the old troll caves."

"You've had another murder?" That was a horrifying thought. I used to believe that small towns were supposed to be safe.

Conall reached for his food again. "It isn't a murder. He

45

looks like a hermit who had been squatting in the old caves and got sick. Nobody was around to help him."

"That's terrible." I exclaimed. "Are there many people like that?"

"We have our share of recluses who want nothing to do with any of the clans. They come in for food every now and again, but they keep to themselves. They see any attempt to help them as interference in their lives and they resent it. We've learned to just let them be."

"But if they need help...?"

"There's always assistance for them." Conall dropped his plate and turned to face me. "Always remember that sometimes it may not seem like it, but this town takes care of its own. In times of trouble most of us pull together."

I really hoped that was true.

8

I woke up the next morning feeling warm and safe. I turned around to find Conall raised on his elbow watching me.

"You know, some people would call that a bit creepy," I said as I tapped my fingers against his chest.

He closed his hand over mine, brought it up to his lips and gently kissed the tips of my fingers. "You slept better last night."

I ducked my head. "I was tired, I didn't sleep too well the night before."

The silence passed between us as we both realized the most likely reason for that was because he hadn't been with me.

"I didn't either," he admitted. "I've got very used to sleeping beside you in a short period of time."

At his admission I had to stop myself from asking a question that had been preying on my mind for a couple of weeks.

I felt Conall tense beside me. "What were you about to say?"

"Nothing." I winced at the fake brightness in my voice.

"Now I know it was important." Conall stroked his hand down my arm. "I need to know when there's something bothering you. I can't fix it unless I know."

"Is there a reason we're not sleeping together?" I couldn't believe I blurted that out. I hadn't realized how much it had been bothering me.

"I have been sleeping with you."

I nudged him. "You know what I mean."

Conall dropped on his back and fixed his gaze on the ceiling. "You mean having sex."

"Yes, I mean, usually that's all that guys want but even though we've shared the bed regularly you haven't made a move. I mean, I understand if you don't want to have sex with me. Well, I don't understand...Are you laughing at me?"

He was. I could feel his shoulders shaking. Tears pricked the back of my eyes and I bolted for the bathroom before I totally humiliated myself. Usually Conall had quicker reflexes, but I must have surprised him because he was a bit slow coming after me. I got to the bathroom and slammed the door shut, put my back against it and slid to the floor, tears streaming down my face as I tried desperately to hold in the noisy sobs that just wanted to come out.

Conall pounded on the door. "Sadie, let me in. I'm sorry. I wasn't laughing at you."

I forced a fake smile on my face. Even if he couldn't see it, I could pretend I wasn't hurting. "That's okay. I just really needed to go to the bathroom. I could be a while. I don't think that Chinese agreed with me. You go to work. I'll see you later." And with that image in his mind I killed any thought of romance between us.

"Sadie, I'm not leaving until you come out."

He severely underestimated my staying ability when it

came to sulking in the bathroom. My mother had learned that lesson early.

"I was just… We're not ready yet." I could hear the frustration in his voice.

"You're absolutely right. I wasn't thinking."

"Sadie, you need to come out now so we can talk about this."

I didn't know how to answer him, and for once the universe was smiling on me because I heard his phone ring. In my experience, when the sheriff's phone rang when he was off-duty, it meant there was a problem that only he could solve.

I could hear his voice low as he talked in the phone. After that came a sharp word that I had never heard him use before.

He tapped on the door again. "Sadie, I have to go but we need to talk about this."

"Of course, have a good day." I cringed at the sound of my fake happy voice.

There was silence and I knew he was fighting the inclination to rip the door off its hinges. I let out my breath when I heard his steps fading away. When the front door closed, I released the stranglehold over the hurt that I was feeling. It took a while to calm down. In my head I knew I was probably overreacting, but at this moment my head wasn't in charge. I went into the shower and let the hot water soothe me.

Half an hour later I made a decision. There was no way I was going to the diner today for breakfast and risk running into the one person I didn't want to speak to. Instead, I grabbed a piece of toast and headed straight for work. When I reached the coven library, I was relieved to feel peace steal over me. Sometimes I imagined that the magic housed within it had given the building a sentience. If so, I had to believe she was happy, and we were working well together. I had two hours before my interview so I figured I could get a good amount of work in. That belief flew out the window when I was surprised by Tilda walking in an hour later.

She pulled out a chair and sat opposite me. "I've been trying to call you. Do you want to tell me what's going on?"

"Not particularly," I replied without looking up from my work.

"Let's see. You're not answering your phone and Karl says that the sheriff is on a tear. Something is going on between you two."

I finally looked up and closed the text I was working on with a heavy thud. "I don't believe it is anybody's business."

"What did that idiot do?"

"Why do you assume it was him?" It was definitely him, but it wasn't fair for Tilda to assume it was him.

"So, it wasn't him?"

"Of course, it was him, but it's not his fault that he doesn't want me." I can't believe I blurted that out.

Tilda put a hand to her forehead. "Let me get this straight. You think that Conall Tolan, who is spending all his time with you and is your Destined Beloved, doesn't want you."

"He doesn't. He's trapped by this thing, but he doesn't really want me."

I could feel the tears welling up again and I ruthlessly willed them away. I was sick of not being good enough.

Tilda looked confused. "Are you talking about sex?"

"Why would I be talking about sex?" Even I could tell from my unnaturally high voice that I was lying to her.

"Have you not had sex yet?" she asked.

"That's none of your business," I replied primly, reaching for another text I could bury myself in and ignore the woman sitting across from me.

"You haven't had sex yet," she concluded correctly. "But

he's always sleeping over at your place. There's been plenty of opportunity."

"And yet no cigar," I said irritably. "Wait a minute, that came out wrong."

"Did he tell you why? I'm sure there has to be a reasonable explanation."

"He laughed." Two words was all it took for the humiliation to come rushing back. The tears started streaming again and I wanted to bury myself in a deep hole.

"Oh, you poor thing." Tilda jumped out of the chair and came around to my side of the table. She put her arms around me and started crooning as if I was a small child.

I gave a watery laugh. "I don't know why I'm so weepy about it. It isn't the first time I've been rejected. In an hour I've got a meeting with the last guy who didn't think I was good enough and ghosted me."

"Men suck," Tilda said, vehemently.

"Yeah," I agreed. "I forgot there for a little while. I just needed a reminder."

"You know what we need?"

I had a feeling this was going to involve a lot of alcohol.

"We need a girl's night out."

And I was right. "Are we taking the Seer bar hopping again?"

"Sure," Tilda said. "Everybody already thinks we're a bad influence on her. Why don't we set that reputation in stone?"

9

*B*y the time Tilda left the library I had barely enough time to grab my things together and get to the meeting hall for my interview. I was relieved to find Tarquin Burroughs waiting for me inside the hall. Tarquin was the coven's advocate. He was also a member of the coven, which was unusual as he was not a witch. He was a vampire. And I felt safer with him than I did my ex-boyfriend. That really said it all about my current life.

"You ready for this?" I asked.

Tarquin groaned. "I've already been through thirteen of them."

I was surprised. "So, they're quick, are they? How long do you think we'll be? Ten, fifteen minutes?"

Tarquin tilted his head from side to side as if trying to remove a kink. "Considering your previous relationship with this particular magister, I think we could be a bit longer than that."

I hoped not. "How did you know about that?"

"I could say that your aunt filled me in."

"You could say?"

"I've a feeling you'd be happier with that answer, but the truth is everybody knows that there used to be something between you and Bernauer. Theories abound as to what it was and how the sheriff is reacting. Everyone is waiting to see the fireworks with bated breath."

That was just super.

"Let's get this stupid meeting done so I can go and do something useful," I grumbled.

"Annoyed and recalcitrant." Tarquin grinned broadly, his fangs on display. "That's the attitude I was looking for. Much better than fearful and defeated."

I gave him a sour look. "Today is not the day to mess with me. I'm skating a very thin line."

Tarquin shrugged. "I can work with that."

My advocate ushered me into a side room of the hall where I found Julian sitting next to Magister Hartford at a table with papers piled neatly on it. Great, I was going to be interviewed by my ex-boyfriend and his fiancée that he neglected to tell me about when we were together. Julian looked at Tarquin with distaste.

"I'm surprised you feel the need for an advocate," he drawled.

I glanced between the two men in confusion. "I thought everybody had an advocate with them. I was told it was required."

"Not required," Tarquin murmured. "Just highly recommended."

"Oh well." I shrugged. "You're here now. You may as well stay." There was no way I was letting Tarquin leave this room without me. I hoped that despite my casual demeanor he understood that.

We took our seats opposite the two magisters and I had to admit the weirdness factor had gone off the scale for my life.

"Sadie, Magister Hartford will be observing the interview

while reading you to ensure complete honesty in all your answers. She will not be speaking to you or asking any questions."

That last bit was said with a frown and seemed to be aimed at the magister more than me. I got the feeling that there had been words regarding Julian's insistence on being the one to interview me.

"Can you please explain to me how you came to live in Walker Bay."

And with that first question I knew that I was in for a long day. Fortunately, Flora and I had practiced our answers to these kinds of questions with the expectation that I was going to be interrogated at some point. We hadn't expected it to be by an ex-boyfriend, but life takes some strange turns at times.

Instead of the knocked out and kidnapped by two little old ladies truth, which was a little embarrassing, I was going with being approached by a senior member of the coven and respectfully asked to assist my aunt in her time of need. I tried to act calm, because this was going to be the moment when I would find out if the legends about magisters not being able to tell if a cursebreaker is lying was true.

"And you dropped your life behind to help a woman you didn't know?" Julian sounded incredulous, and I didn't blame him.

"She's the only family I have and she was in trouble. I couldn't turn my back on her."

Julian's eyes softened. I did not want him to do that. It was one thing for him to believe my lies. It was another for him to pity me.

"You got to Walker Bay and what happened next?"

"We soon discovered that it was not an illness. Fortunately, my aunt found a way to communicate with me through my dreams. From there we discovered she had been cursed. The coven then turned its attentions to finding the curse and breaking it."

"The coven claims it was successful." Julian didn't sound so sure.

"Yes. After the curse was broken it was discovered that Isobel Fulton was responsible. She tried to cast a second one and it backfired on her."

Julian looked through his notes. "According to what I've heard you were not with the coven when they were doing the ritual."

I gave a small smile. "I may have known about the paranormal world, but I had no training. At that point I was useless to the coven. I preferred to sit with my aunt as she seemed to be fading. I was afraid she would not last long enough for the curse to be broken."

I kept my eyes on Julian, trying desperately to ignore the woman sitting next to him with the unblinking stare.

Julian leaned back in his chair and studied me. "Why do you think Isobel Fulton strayed so far from the coven?"

I shrugged, wondering why he would ask something like that. "I didn't know her at all. I wouldn't even like to hazard a guess as to why she did something so horrendous to her friend."

"According to reports you were also kidnapped by the werewolf who murdered Jeanette Hocking."

I nodded. "Brian Tolan wanted to hurt his brother. He believed killing me was the best way to accomplish that goal."

"Your Destined Beloved?"

"Yes," I answered shortly. I was seriously beginning to hate that term. I wish Agnes had never had that prophecy.

"And your Destined Beloved saved your life and almost killed his own brother."

I cannot tell you how annoyed I was that I had to defend him today. "The sheriff did his job and apprehended a murderer. Jeanette died in a horrific manner. Justice was served in difficult circumstances."

Julian's eyes gleamed and my breath caught in my throat. I had given something away and I had no idea what it was.

"There are many in the coven who are concerned by the Destined Beloved prophecy between a berserker werewolf and a candidate for the coven leadership."

I didn't think anything could make me laugh today, but Julian had accomplished it. It wasn't a dainty laugh either. I laughed so hard it actually hurt. Julian and Magister Hartford stared at me as I tried to calm myself down. "That was funny," I wheezed as I wiped tears from my eyes.

Julian leaned forward against the table. "Coven leadership has a tendency to go through bloodlines. As far as I can see you're the prime candidate.

I pulled my troll doll out of my bag and slammed it down on the table in front of him. "This is my privacy spell. It is the only spell I have been able to learn so far and it took me an embarrassingly long time to accomplish it. I have only been able to do it on the doll. Every time I try it on something else I fail. The chances of me becoming the next coven leader are as likely as that doll coming alive and becoming president. Whether I'm part of a prophecy or not doesn't matter. At best I will be an adequate witch, destined to languish in the background. There is no chance that I am ever going to be the coven leader. Anyone who tells you otherwise is deluded." I grabbed my troll doll back and jammed it in my bag. "Now please, could we keep the questions to situations which are slightly less fantastical."

I could see the amusement in Julian's eyes, but there was also something else. I was hoping it was respect. "Very well, let's go over your story again."

For the next several hours Julian questioned me repeatedly about my role in the coven and the various incidents that had happened in Walker Bay since I'd arrived, all under the glare of his fiancée. By the time we were finished I felt wrung out. I was pretty sure he believed everything that I had told him, or at least I hoped so.

Julian stood up and came around to my side of the table. "I need to do a truth spell on you."

I pulled back. "What are you talking about?"

"Don't worry, it's a standard spell after an interview. It doesn't hurt at all. Just a way of confirming all the information that you gave me was correct."

"That's not necessary," Magister Hartford said through gritted teeth. "I have been reading her the entire time and she is telling the truth."

I had to stop myself from breathing a sigh of relief. It seemed that those old legends about cursebreakers being able to lie with impunity were true. Yay for me.

The look Julian sent his fiancée's way was withering. "Nonetheless, I will be doing a truth spell."

I glanced over at Tarquin and caught his nod. I still didn't like the fact that it was happening, but if he didn't have any qualms about it, I guess I didn't have a choice.

I nodded sharply.

He arranged the chairs so that we sat opposite each other, so close our knees were touching. He put his hands on both sides of my face and stared deeply into my eyes. Words could not describe how uncomfortable I felt, especially as I could feel Hartford's glare boring into the side of my head.

"Is everything you have told me today the truth?"

"Yes." I figured short and sharp was the best way to go. At this point there was nothing else I could do. I had spent the last few hours tap dancing around the truth. The only way forward was to continue on the path laid out for me.

"Have you hidden any information that would assist this investigation?"

"No."

"Is there anything that you are keeping from me?"

"No."

"Do you love your Destined Beloved?"

"And we're done." I grabbed his wrists and yanked them away from my head. I then stood so quickly that I caused my chair to be knocked over. I would have gone over too in my scramble to get away if it hadn't been for Tarquin grabbing my arms to keep me upright and pulling me away from the man I now wanted to brain with the chair. I glanced up to find anger radiating from my advocate, his fangs bared.

"That was extraordinarily unprofessional," he hissed.

Julian leaned back and smiled, not at all concerned that he now had a vampire who looked like he wanted to tear his throat out. "Actually, it wasn't. I was just wondering what her response would have been to that question. A lot of people are compelled to answer under that particular spell. I find it interesting that you weren't. You may just be stronger than you think."

My stomach clenched with fear at the speculative gleam in his eyes.

"If I'm to be questioned again, send Magister Rigby. I refuse to speak to you." I picked up my bag and stalked out of the room.

I was surprised to find Flora waiting for me in the main hall.

"What did he do?" Her voice was low and threatening, and she looked like a mama bear ready to pounce to defend her cub.

I wasn't quite ready to talk so I was fortunate that Tarquin jumped in. "He asked about her relationship with the sheriff while under the truth spell."

Flora closed her eyes. "He's not supposed to do that."

"Well, he did, and I will by filing a complaint about it."

I could see that Tarquin meant to do the right thing, but I didn't want to call any more attention to myself than I already had.

"No, just leave it be for now."

Tarquin frowned. "Are you sure? I don't care what his reasoning was. He shouldn't have done that."

I nodded sharply. "I'm sure. I just want to forget this day happened. With any luck I won't have to deal with him again."

Flora put her hand on Tarquin's arm. "Thank you so much for taking care of her. It means a great deal to me." Tarquin looked down at her and she glanced away as she pulled her hand back. For the first time I saw a chink in Tarquin's armor as a very pale reddish flush stole across his cheeks. Who would have thought that a vampire could blush? I glanced over at Flora and saw she was desperately looking everywhere but at the man who was now watching her with unabashed devotion. Oh, wow. I had not been expecting this.

Tarquin cleared his throat. "I will let you know when the interviews are finished. You will have a report outlining questions asked and my opinion on future actions."

Flora clasped her hands together and nodded, carefully avoiding Tarquin's gaze.

"Thank you. Your assistance is very much appreciated."

Tarquin nodded sharply and headed back into the room with Julian and Magister Hartford. I had a feeling any good-will he'd had for those two had just gone up in smoke.

I waited until he left and we were walking outside before nudging my aunt.

"Did you want to tell me what that was all about?"

Flora didn't even look back at me as she headed for her car. "No."

Once I got in my own vehicle, I realized that I had a problem. My emotions were still pretty wired, so the last thing I

needed was to run into Conall. My chances of further humiliating myself were pretty high. I needed to find somewhere
for the day to hunker down and get myself back on an even
emotional keel before I could face him. I felt myself smile as
an option came to mind. I started the engine and went to the
one place I was pretty sure the sheriff wouldn't come for me.

10

"What are you doing here?"

As far as greetings were concerned, it wasn't the best, but I'd worked with less. I put on a big smile. "I just thought I'd come over and spend time with you before we went out tonight."

"I'm the Seer," Agnes said, sourly. "That means I'm smarter than the average witch. You're hiding out from your Destined Beloved and your ex-boyfriend."

Fine, I'd go with honesty. "Yes, I am. I'm having a day where I'm not particularly fond of men and it seems that your place is the only man-free zone in this town. Since I'm in this mess because of you, I figure the least you could do is provide sanctuary."

Agnes sighed heavily and opened her door wider. "Fine, you can come in until we go out." She picked up her phone and started texting.

"What are you doing?"

"I'm letting Tilda know that she needs to come and pick us both up." The reply came back almost immediately. "She'll be here in an hour."

Agnes sat on her couch and tucked her knees under herself. "So, did you want to fill me in on why you're messing with my prophecy?"

I flopped down on a chair opposite her. "Because that's what I seem to do. For some reason I don't really inspire great devotion in men." I couldn't believe it when tears started welling up in my eyes and I waved my hands at my face. "See this, I am not normally this weepy. For some reason I'm feeling embarrassed and rejected. Like I'm not good enough. That's what men have done to me today. It's ticking me off." I wiped at my eyes angrily.

Agnes peered at me with sympathy in her eyes. "I think I know what you need."

"What I need is to not have to deal with men for one night," I grumbled.

"We're not staying here for the night," Agnes said darkly. "Do you know how rare it is for me to go out? I'm not missing it because you're having a meltdown."

"Great, we'll make it all about you," I said, trying my best to smile. "What is your suggestion then?"

"I think you need a makeover."

"That is the stupidest idea ever," I said, "and I should know because stupid ideas seem to be my specialty these days."

"Will it make you feel worse?" Agnes challenged.

I shrugged. "Maybe, maybe not."

Agnes obviously took that as an acceptance of her plan because she clapped her hands. "I've never done a makeover on someone. Don't worry, this will be fun."

I somehow doubted it.

An hour later, Tilda walked into the house and stopped suddenly at the sight of me. "Oh, wow."

"And I'm getting changed." I went to grab some of my clothes that Agnes had deemed unsuitable. Instead she'd dressed me in tight jeans and a button up top that although it wasn't skintight, managed to show my curves off to great effect. The outfit was not overly risqué, but it was different to what I would normally wear.

Tilda put out her hands as if to stop me. "No, you look great. You just don't look like someone in a committed relationship."

"I'm not in a committed relationship. I'm sharing a bed with a man who refuses to have sex with me, even though he's slept with pretty much the rest of the female population in this town." As I said the words, I realized they were true. That's what was wrong with me. Conall might not have meant to do it, but he'd managed to expose every single insecurity I had about not being good enough. Having Julian turning up just helped amplify the problem. Man, that sucked.

"Just tell me I don't look ridiculous," I said quietly. "I just can't handle any more humiliation today."

The two women who were fast becoming the closest friends I had ever had hurriedly assured me that I wasn't going to embarrass myself. Tilda tweaked a few of the details where Agnes may have gone overboard. After a bit more work they both declared that I was ready to face the world, or at least the crowd at the local bar.

By the time we arrived at our destination, the two women had me laughing hilariously as they related ridiculous stories of life in Walker Bay. We managed to grab one of the tables and ordered some food and drinks.

Tilda raised her eyebrow when my mocktail turned up. "I would have thought that tonight would be the perfect time for something with a little more kick."

"It probably would be," I took a sip of the way too sweet concoction. "But I've learned from painful experience that alcohol is not my friend. Sugar is my vice tonight."

Tilda shrugged and went back to her drink. "Your choice."

After we'd finished our food Agnes slapped her hands on the table. "I want to dance."

I choked on my drink. "You're kidding, aren't you?" I gestured to the dance floor where two lonely souls were attempting to line dance.

"I've never danced in my life. I want to dance."

When she put it like that. "You don't by any chance know how to line dance, do you?" I asked Tilda.

Tilda dropped her head. "I do. My mother needed somebody to go with her to lessons, and I drew the short straw.

Agnes jumped up and grabbed our hands, dragging us to the dance floor. She and I stood just behind Tilda, prepared to learn a new skill.

"I can't believe I'm doing this," she muttered as she started doing steps, slowly and deliberately to allow us to follow.

Agnes and I tried to keep up, but we were woefully ill-equipped for the challenge presented to us. I spent most of my time with my eyes glued to Tilda and had a tendency to take bigger steps than necessary. Agnes took the basics of what Tilda was trying to show us and added her own flair. The result was an ungainly mess that culminated in Agnes and I running into each other and ending up in a tangle of limbs on the ground, laughing at our complete lack of coordination.

Tilda grabbed a hand from each of us and hauled us to a standing position. "I can't believe how bad you guys are."

I was still laughing as I glanced over at the bar, only to sober when I realized we had an audience. "I'm going to sit the next one out," I muttered.

Tilda and Agnes followed my gaze and nodded in agreement.

"Sorry, guys," I said. "I just didn't expect both of them to be here.

I had not imagined I would look up and see Julian and Conall both sitting at the bar. Not together of course. Conall was at one end of the bar with his brother Eamon, the only member of his family that he could tolerate. Julian was at the other end of the bar with both Magister Rigby and Magister Hartford, who once again was looking at me as if I was evil incarnate. Both of the groups were as far apart from each other as they could get, but both Julian and Conall made no secret of the fact that they were staring at me as I made a fool of myself on the dance floor. I mentally shrugged. Despite my complete lack of coordination, I had been having fun. I realized that it had been a long time since I had just done something for fun. I frowned trying to remember the last time. When had I lost that side of me?

Tilda touched my arm. "Are you okay?"

I looked up to see both she and Agnes had identical worried expressions. I smiled in the face of my friends' concern. "I'm fine, in fact, I'm having a great time." I grabbed a bartender and ordered another drink. "I was just trying to remember the last time I had so much fun. It's been a while," I admitted.

"Maybe we should try dancing again," ventured Tilda, although I could see she was loath to get back out on the dance floor.

I laughed at her expression. "I think it might be worth us getting lessons before we try that again. That and a medical kit. I think I have injuries from hitting the floor."

"What are you talking about?" groused Agnes. "I was the one who copped your knee in my side."

The joy I felt as the three of us joked and teased each other was something that had been missing from my life for a long time. I couldn't believe I had let myself get so serious. My mother would be horrified. She and I used to end up on the floor howling with laughter over ridiculous things. When she'd died it seems I'd buried that capacity for joy with her. I was grateful that these two women had helped me find it again.

"Excuse me, ladies."

We looked up to find a well-dressed man smiling at Agnes, his eyes glued to the young Seer.

"I was wondering if you'd like to dance."

"What, me?" The look of panic on Agnes's face was priceless. "Uh, I don't…"

"She'd love to," Tilda interrupted smoothly, her hand discreetly under Agnes's elbow, lifting her up from the table.

"Are you sure?" hissed Agnes.

"Absolutely," I replied.

We watched as the two headed for the dance floor.

"You know, we are always going to be known as the ones who corrupted a Seer," I said conversationally as we watched Agnes nervously trying to follow the moves of her partner.

Tilda waved her hand in the air. "I've gone past the point of caring."

We both winced as Agnes stepped on her partner's foot.

"You were right to ask her out that first time." I was surprised to hear Tilda say that. As I recall, she was horrified by my impulsive invitation to the Seer. "It's not right that she stays virtually locked up her whole life."

"So, we're going to stand with her against any backlash?" I queried, putting my hand out.

"Absolutely." She grasped my hand and we both smiled.

"Would you like to dance, Tilda?"

A part of me was surprised that Magister Rigby was asking Tilda to dance. Remembering her comment about him being hot, I interrupted her before she could refuse him.

"Of course, she'll dance with you." I lowered my voice. "Have fun, I'll wait for you here."

She looked rebellious, although I could see a part of her wanted to take up the invitation.

"Go," I encouraged, shooing her with my hands. "Make sure Agnes hasn't permanently maimed her partner."

Despite her reluctance, Tilda took the hand of the magister and let herself be led to the dance floor.

I smiled as I watched my two friends. I knew there was no chance of anyone asking me to dance. Not with Conall glaring at anyone coming near our table. Nobody in this town was that much of an idiot.

"May I have this dance?"

Correction. Almost nobody in this town was that much of an idiot. "You do realize you are going to get yourself killed," I remarked, ignoring Julian's outstretched hand.

"A dance with you would be worth it." And there was that charming grin, the one I'd fallen for.

I smiled up at him. "I'm not dancing with you. To do so in this town, in front of him and your fiancée would be disrespectful. I'm not doing that."

Julian slid into the seat recently vacated by Tilda. "I didn't think so, but I figured I should try."

"I don't recall inviting you to sit with me."

Julian's eyes widened innocently. "I'm just protecting your virtue by discouraging potential suitors."

I couldn't help it. I laughed. I really didn't want to, but the thought of Julian being on the side of angels was more than I could cope with.

"So how long are we going to be blessed with your company in our fair town," I asked as I played with my glass.

"There's a lot to do," Julian said calmly. "I could be in town for a while, and I do have family here."

"Yes," I drawled. "Next time I see Violet I'll have to ask about her career as a stripper."

Julian choked on his drink and started coughing. "Aah,

yes. I was a little creative with the truth when we were together."

"I'll say," I said casually. "I seem to remember that you were following in your father's footsteps and working in the banking industry."

He tilted his head. "I did follow my father's footsteps. He's one of the members of the Conclave. Becoming a magister is generally the first step on that path."

I barely managed to keep my expression calm at that piece of news. Yet another reason for me to stay as far away from Julian as I could. Not that I needed one.

Julian put his glass down and focused on me. "I've been speaking to a friend who has done research into the Destined Beloved prophecy."

I put up a hand. "I really don't think you want to continue going down that path," I warned.

Naturally, Julian ignored me. "He says there are ways to break the link. Free you of a tradition that's little more than an arranged marriage." I thought that was rich coming from a man who was heading for an arranged marriage based on family ambition.

And that was as far as Julian got before he was yanked off his chair by Conall and passed on to Eamon who hustled him back to the bar.

I waved at my friends who were pulling away from their dance partners to come to my defense to let them know I was fine.

"You lasted longer than I thought you would," I remarked, knowing that Conall had used that super werewolf hearing of his to listen to every word that had been said at this table.

"We need to talk," he gritted out.

"Then talk." I was surprised by how calmly I was dealing with both Julian and Conall. It looked like I'd cooled down from the weepy mess I'd been earlier in the day.

"Not here." He looked around. "I want to talk in private."

I looked at my empty glass and for the first time wished I'd gone for something stronger. I knew how stubborn Conall could be. I wasn't going to get back to my girl's night until we'd hashed out our issues.

"You have five minutes."

I knew that Tilda and Agnes weren't happy at the sight of me following Conall into the office. I shook my head at them to stop them from coming to my rescue. The office looked the same as it did the last time we'd had one of our talks, and I wondered whether it was used for anything else. I'd never seen anyone actually go into it. I turned and clasped my hands together in front of me, carefully controlling my breathing.

"What do you want to talk about?"

For a moment Conall looked lost. "I wanted to apologize about this morning. I wasn't laughing at you. I was laughing at myself and the situation we find ourselves in."

"Julian's right, isn't he? It's like an arranged marriage." I shook my head. "Things have been so intense that it didn't really register that I barely know you." I took a deep breath and hoped that I could get through the next minute with the least amount of humiliation possible. "I apologize for trying to pressure you into something you're clearly not wanting."

Conall growled. "You've got it all wrong. It's not that I don't want to take that step with you, I just don't think we're ready for it."

I was careful not to let my smile slip. "Thank you for clearing that up. After thinking about it today, I agree with you. It's just difficult when I spend my day surrounded by or getting sneered at by women that you were ready for. The fact that you're reluctant to take that step with me has brought up issues that I thought I'd dealt with. Maybe Julian being here has exacerbated the situation." I twisted my hands nervously. I knew I wasn't explaining this well, and I just wanted him to go before I broke down again. "I really have to get back to my friends."

I went to move past him only to have him catch my arm. "I'll see you at your place tonight. We can talk some more."

I shook my head. "No, I'd rather you not come over anymore. You being in my bed is confusing the issue. I think you were right the other day. We need some space. I want to look into the Destined Beloved prophecy. I think we may have accepted it too fast without researching our options."

I slipped around him and made my way out of the office before I said or did something truly stupid. When I got back to the table where Tilda and Agnes were waiting expectantly, I let out the breath I had been holding.

Tilda glanced past my shoulder. "That doesn't look like it went well."

I resisted the urge to turn around and find out what she was seeing.

"We're not talking about it." I was resolved. I did need a bit of time. The fact that I was reacting so badly to Conall meant that I had not dealt with any of my baggage from my time with Julian. Nothing good would happen if we just tried continuing on our way without addressing the real issues.

I put a smile on my face. "So, how did the dancing go after I got dragged away?"

Agnes rolled her eyes. "I think I broke him."

I grinned. "I'm sure that's not true."

"He was limping when he brought me back here." Her tone was mournful.

"Did you have fun?"

Agnes nodded shyly.

"Then his sacrifice has not been in vain."

Tilda laughed as she ordered another drink.

"And how was your dance with the magister?

"Fine," she said shortly.

"Not interested in sharing?"

"Not particularly."

I could respect that. Sometimes you just needed some time to work things out in your own head before sharing them with the world.

11

"We really need to do this again," I gasped as I dropped heavily in my seat. Once Conall and Julian had left the bar I had been able to lose some of the tension that had been riding me and decided dancing was a skill I needed to learn.

"No, we don't," Tilda replied.

As she had been the one who had tried to teach two rhythmically challenged women how to line dance for the past two hours, and failed completely, I could understand her attitude.

I glanced over at Agnes and was about to make a joke at our expense when I noticed her expression.

"What's wrong?"

"You need to get me out of here, right now," Agnes gasped, her face ghostly pale.

Tilda and I rushed to her side and started leading her out of the bar. As we stepped outside the door she dropped like a stone and the dead weight almost dragged the two of us to the ground. We each looped an arm around our necks and half dragged, half carried her to the car.

"What's going on?" I asked as Tilda unlocked the vehicle.

"I think she's having a vision."

We lowered her in the front seat and ensured she stayed upright. I kept glancing at her, terrified that at any moment she was going to have a seizure.

"What do we do?" I felt useless watching our friend going through something we could not understand.

Tilda shrugged helplessly. "I have no idea. She's usually alone when she has visions."

"We need to take her to a doctor."

"No, you don't." Agnes raised her hand to her head.

"Thank the Fates," Tilda breathed.

"What happened?" I asked, a bit more demanding than I meant to. "One minute you were fine and the next you were out for the count."

Agnes ignored my question. "Trouble's coming."

"How bad?" Tilda asked grimly.

"Bad."

Tilda rolled her shoulders. "We'll get you home and then call the coven leader so you can warn her."

"I think it might be too late," whispered Agnes.

We headed for Agnes's house and I called Flora.

"She's not going to be happy about this," muttered Tilda.

I knew that, but I couldn't find it within myself to regret the night we'd had.

Tilda was right. Flora wasn't happy that we'd once again taken the Seer out for the night, but there wasn't much she could say in the face of Agnes's defiance. What she could do was send us home before we heard what the prophecy was. According to Flora, the Seer's message had to come through the coven leader, and nothing was going to change that.

~

THERE'S nothing quite like a vision of impending doom to put a dampener on a great night out. That wasn't helped by the moonless night that seemed to close in on me as I walked into an empty house. I checked the doors twice before I headed up to bed. I hadn't even made it to my bedroom when there was a pounding on my front door.

Fully believing it to be either Julian or Conall, I ripped open the door. It wasn't who I was expecting.

"Help me, please."

None of my neighbors had made an effort to introduce themselves to me, so I was surprised to find the elderly guy from next door leaning against the door jamb. The most I'd seen of him were the disapproving looks he had given me when Conall left some mornings.

"What happened?" I quickly looked him over, fully expecting to see blood. "I'll call the police."

"No." He reached out his hand to stop me. "I need a doctor. Feel sick."

I had no idea how the emergency services in this town worked and I figured at this time of night I'd be quicker bundling him in the car and taking him to Dr Collias myself. I scooped up my keys and helped him walk to my car.

"I'll get you to the clinic," I soothed as I loaded him into the car, grabbing a vomit bag out of the glove compartment and passing it to him. As a non-drinker I had been designated the driver on many an outing. I had learned early to take precautions.

It didn't take us long to get to Dr Collias' house. I was surprised to see lights glowing from every window.

"Looks like something's going on," I murmured.

I unloaded my neighbor who was now leaning heavily onto me and headed for the front door. I hit the bell and leaned against the wall next to it, ensuring I was still supporting the man who barely seemed conscious. His face was a pasty white and when I put a hand to his forehead, he felt clammy.

After what seemed like hours the door opened, and Dr Collias poked his head out.

"Sadie, what are you doing here?"

I tried to straighten up, but the weight of my neighbor kept me pushed against the wall. It was like he was no longer able to stand. I indicated my problem. "He just turned up on my porch. I think he's my neighbor. I was afraid he was having a heart attack."

"I wish," muttered Dr Collias as he started a cursory examination under the porch light. He must have seen my raised eyebrow because he hastily tried to reassure me. "I don't mean that the way it sounded. I've just had a few people turn up tonight with these symptoms and I don't know yet what is going on. Come with me." I was shocked when he effortlessly scooped my neighbor into his arms and started heading into the clinic. Maybe I shouldn't have been surprised. After all, he was centaur. I'd assume some extra strength came with the rest of the package. I dutifully followed him, not sure what he wanted me to do.

"Wait here," he barked, and I obediently sat down in the waiting area.

After half an hour, Dr Collias walked into the waiting room and wiped his hand over his face. "Come into the examination room." I followed him in thinking that he was going to talk to me about my neighbor. "I need you to take off your shirt."

I raised an eyebrow and stared at him, waiting for an explanation. I was not the sort of girl who acquiesced to an order like that without a really good reason.

"That came out wrong," he sighed.

"I'm glad that you're still able to recognize that," I replied.

"Your neighbor has taken ill with what looks like a virus. I currently have several people in here with the same thing. Symptoms include nausea, chills, swollen joints, muscle aches and lethargy. Normally I would assume it was the flu, but all of them have presented with welts on the chest."

I looked down my top. "No welts."

"I'll take your word for it," he said dryly.

"I'm not giving you a choice," I retorted.

"I'll keep William overnight." He must have seen my confused expression. "Your neighbor's name is William. You might want to start getting to know some of the people who live near you."

"I'll take that under advisement. Do you need any help?" I offered.

He shook his head. "I think we've got it covered." He straightened up. "Keep an eye on yourself for any strange symptoms. I have no idea how contagious this thing is."

Well, that was a pleasant thought. As my mother always used to say, no good deed ever goes unpunished.

*T*he next morning I decided that I would do my good deed for the day and offer to drive my neighbor home. Maybe that would improve the man's opinion of me. When I reached the clinic there seemed to be more cars than I would have expected for a weekend. I followed a worried looking ogre into the building and found a scene of utter chaos. There were people shouting at the receptionist, demanding to see the doctor. Others were sitting in the chairs, barely conscious, worried family members holding them upright.

I skirted the group and headed for the room I knew that William had been put in the night before. I noticed the coven healer Marigold in a side room, grinding something in a stone bowl so I popped my head in.

"What's going on?"

Marigold jumped. "Oh, Sadie. I didn't notice you there." A look of panic crossed her features. "You're not sick, are you?"

I shook my head. "No, I brought my neighbor in last night. Dr Collias was going to keep him in overnight for observation. I just thought I'd come and offer him a ride home."

Marigold smiled. "That's lovely. Who is it?"

I could feel my cheeks redden. "I don't really know his full name, we haven't had anything to do with each other until he knocked on my door last night. I think Dr Collias said his name was William. And before you say anything, I'm going to make a better effort at getting to know my neighbors, starting with William."

Marigold's expression was stricken. "I'm sorry, Sadie. William died a few hours ago."

That didn't sound right. "Are you sure you have the right William? He was just in here overnight for a virus, like the flu."

"We don't know what's happening. Perfectly healthy men in the town are coming down with it. We've lost three already."

"Has his family been told?"

Marigold started grinding again. "William didn't have any family. He barely had anything to do with the coven. He was always a bit of a loner. That's probably why he came to you for help last night. He had nobody else."

That was sad. "Is there any chance I could see him?" I asked.

"Why would you want to do that?"

I could see her frown and knew her first inclination would be to say no. To be honest, I wasn't sure why I felt the need to see the body of a man I didn't know, but it was like something else was driving me to do it.

"I just want to say goodbye, and to let him know that somebody cares that he died." I shrugged sheepishly. "I know it sounds silly."

Marigold's expression softened. She stood up and put her hand on my arm. "It doesn't sound silly. Come with me."

She took me downstairs to the basement before I could rethink this idea. Although it was brighter than I expected, it still rated highly on the creepiness factor, especially when you took into account the three bodies that were lying on tables in the center of the room.

Marigold stepped towards one and lowered the sheet so I could see his face. "I'll give you a few minutes," Marigold said before heading back up the stairs, leaving me alone in the morgue.

I looked down at the face of the man who I had only met twelve hours earlier. I wanted to say something profound, something to mark his passing. I had nothing. I was about to give up and go back upstairs when I noticed movement underneath the sheet. I watched frozen as something seemed to be sliding up the body, towards William's exposed face.

Every instinct in me screamed that I should be running, but I was frozen on the spot. Finally, whatever it was poked out from the top of the sheet and wrapped around his chin. The sad thing was that I felt relief at the sight of the tendrils that were becoming all too familiar to me. I tentatively put out my hand and touched it, thankful when it disintegrated. I pulled the sheet back and gasped at the sight of more of the tendrils wound tightly into a knot on top of William's chest. With a feeling of dread, I pulled back the sheets on the other two men and found the same thing. I got my phone out and called the one person who would know what to do.

"I need help," I whispered when my aunt answered the phone.

"Where are you?"

"The morgue at the clinic. You need to get here now. I think I know what Agnes saw last night and she was right. This is bad."

≈

THE TIME between that phone call and hearing Flora's footsteps coming down the stairs seemed endless. I was relieved to see her alone.

"I'd make a joke about you seeing a ghost, but considering where you're standing, that might be a little inappropriate."

"I wish it was a ghost." I pointed to William. "What do you see when you look at him?"

Flora frowned. "I see a dead man."

I pointed again. "On his chest, what do you see on his chest?"

Flora stepped over to the table. "He has welts on his chest. I've never seen anything like it. They look like they would hurt."

"I see a clump of tendrils curled together so tightly it's like they are knotted together, and they won't move for anyone."

"Are you telling me this is a curse?" Flora's voice wavered, and I didn't blame her.

"I'm saying that each of these three men has that same knot of tendrils that looks like the other curses that I have worked with."

"Have you checked any of the ones upstairs?" Flora asked.

"Because that wouldn't look suspicious at all," I said with a healthy dose of sarcasm. "I need to see their chests to see if they're the same. I can't just walk up there and start ripping people's shirts open."

"We only need a few to confirm this is what we think it is." Flora straightened her shoulders. "Leave it to me."

If ever I had any doubts about the power Flora had in this town, the next few minutes blew them away completely. It took less than ten minutes for her to completely clear the clinic of everyone but patients. Even Dr Collias consented to confine himself to his laboratory at the back of the clinic.

We went to the room where the doctor had told us the

worst of the cases were.

"They all have the welts," Flora murmured.

"That's not what I'm seeing," I replied. What I was seeing was a tight, writhing knot of darkness on each of the patient's chests.

"Can you do anything about it?"

I was already reaching for the closest patient. I put my hand on top of the clump and started pulling the tendrils off. I was thankful to see them disintegrate as my hands touched them. Once the last of them was gone I took a closer look at the patient.

"He seems to be breathing better. Maybe it helped."

Flora peered down. "The welts don't look as angry either." She glanced over at me. "Do you think you can do the same thing with the others?"

I nodded and headed for the next patient.

A half hour later I pulled the last tendril from the final patient and sighed with relief.

Flora placed a hand on my forehead. "Are you okay? You're looking pale."

"It takes a little out of me." To be honest, it took a lot out of me, but each of the patients seemed to be breathing better and weren't as clammy as when I first started. I was disappointed that they were all still unconscious.

A deep voice came from the doorway. "I've given you some time Flora, but I need to see to my patients."

Flora turned to face the doctor. "I've finished, Ambrose."

Dr Collias walked over to his closest patient. "They seem better."

Flora fixed a smile to her face. "We've been able to give them some relief but that is all we could do.

Collias shook his head. "It's a curse, isn't it?"

Flora looked surprised. "What makes you say that? Most doctors would not even entertain the possibility."

"I'm not most doctors." Collias crossed his arms across his chest. "When I check their blood there is nothing to indicate an illness. According to every test that I have run, these patients are strong and healthy, and yet every one of them is unconscious. Also, we have the indisputable fact that one hundred percent of the patients are male. Not many viruses discriminate along gender lines. You were recently the victim of a curse. History generally tells us that once one curse has been cast, others follow along behind.

"We think it might be," confirmed Flora. "Normally it wouldn't be my first or even my twentieth guess, but we're living in strange times."

"What can we do?" I couldn't help but notice the haggard appearance of the doctor. This was not a man used to being in a no-win situation.

"Until we find who did this there is very little we can do." Despite her calm stance I could tell that Flora was angry. "We can't let the general public know we have a curse, there will be panic."

"We need to contact the sheriff." Doctor Collias's tone brooked no argument.

While he made the call, I pulled Flora aside. "I don't think I'm any more use here. I want to do some research. See if there's anything else I can do."

Flora nodded sharply. "The sooner we can destroy this thing, the better."

I gave her a quick hug. "Be strong, I'll be at the library if you need me."

When I went to pull away, Flora held on to me. "Just be careful. The magisters will be all over this. Any unusual behavior will be scrutinized. I don't want them to have any reason to look in your direction."

I squeezed her back. I was in complete agreement with that sentiment.

he day passed quickly as I devoured history books with information about curses and illnesses. The more I discovered the more concerned I became. Eventually, I closed the last book and headed home. I couldn't bring myself to eat anything, so I made my way to my deck and sat in the darkness, my back against the wall with my head resting on my knees. The thoughts racing through my head were making me physically sick. I heard the door from my bedroom open and I looked up.

"What are you doing out here, this deck is a death trap."

Flora looked horrified that I was being so careless with my life. I could see the humor in that statement, considering she was my landlord and therefore responsible for the condition of this deck.

"It's okay if you stay close to the edge. The woods rotted more in the middle."

I dropped my head back to my knees.

Flora touched my arm gently as she sat down next to me. "What's wrong?"

I turned my head to the side. I wanted to see her reaction

when I asked this question. "Did I do this? Did I create this curse?"

"Why would you think that?"

I swallowed, trying desperately to dislodge the thick feeling in my throat. "Some of the reading I did today talked about people like me and the fact they were able to cast curses using their own bodies as a medium. I've been pretty angry at men the last couple of days. I've felt rejected and humiliated, and I've had some not very nice thoughts." I turned my face away and looked out over the edge of the deck. I didn't want to see disappointment coming from the one person I wanted to make proud of me. "You said that people like me caused the Black Death plague in Europe that wiped out a good proportion of humans. Is it possible I have that kind of power in me?"

"Yes," she said simply, "it is possible you have that power."

I felt sick.

She cupped her hand under my chin and turned my face towards her. "You may have the power, but I truly believe that you are too strong and too good to be corrupted by it. There is no way that you did this."

I felt hope for the first time. "Are you sure? I was thinking some really horrible things about Conall and Julian."

Flora chuckled quietly. "None of us are saints. We all have those thoughts, especially about the men in our lives. Even though you have the power to cast something like this without having to use a tablet or any of the other accoutrements that most witches have to use, you do still need to sacrifice some of your soul. That is not an easy thing to do. It takes a bit more than a simple thought fueled by anger."

I felt better. All day I had gradually been talking myself into the possibility that I had somehow caused this. It made me feel better that somewhere in Walker Bay there was somebody willing to sacrifice part of their soul to curse a bunch of men. At least it wasn't me.

"What happened after I left? Has anybody else come in?"

Flora nodded regretfully. "More men came in throughout the day. I'm taking you down again tomorrow morning and we'll do a ritual to cover your thing." She waved her hands in the air as if trying to imitate my plucking and shaking of disintegrating tendrils.

"Do I really look that ridiculous when I do it?" I asked, curiosity getting the better of me.

"Pretty much."

I'd have to work on that.

"Any ideas how I go about breaking this curse when we will have the whole town watching, including the Conclave?" I tried to phrase my question lightly, but I knew we were wandering into risky territory.

"We let the sheriff do his job." Flora was decisive. "We have no idea who did this, and until we do there is nothing that can be done. Your contribution is to keep these men alive until Conall can work out who is behind this."

"And I need to do that without anyone catching on."

Flora grinned. "I didn't say it was going to be easy. Did your reading turn anything up?"

"A lot of nightmare situations. I focused on history books after what you told me about cursebreakers causing the Black Death plague. From what I can tell, a curse like this isn't random. It has to be keyed into something common about each person."

"At the moment they are all men."

"It's got to be more than that or every single man would be infected. There has to be something about these men that binds them together."

Flora looked thoughtful. "On the surface the only thing

they have in common is their gender. There weren't only witches in there. I saw a werewolf, an ogre…"

"The giant," I murmured.

"So, it isn't limited by race," Flora mused. "The men I saw today wouldn't generally have anything in common. As far as I know, they don't belong to the same groups, they have different professions, their family lives are different. Some were born here, some weren't. Some are new to town. Some have lived here their whole lives." She shook her head slightly. "We can't get off track. Those are questions for the sheriff. We need to focus on keeping them alive.

She patted me on the knee as she went to stand up. "You need to get some sleep. I've got a bad feeling that you're not going to get much rest over the next few days. I'll pick you up first thing in the morning and we'll go to the clinic to help any others that have come in."

"How are we going to explain what we're doing?"

"I'm the coven leader. If I say that I have a ritual which will ease suffering, nobody is going to question it."

"And what about me?" I queried. "If we're talking power levels here I'm not exactly in your league, or have you forgotten the privacy spell debacle."

Flora wrinkled her nose as if I'd just said something distasteful. "We really need to do something about that troll thing. It's not very dignified."

"I like it," I said defensively. "More importantly, I'm proud of it. At least it's a skill that doesn't have a death sentence attached to it."

Flora patted me on the arm. "I'm sorry, I shouldn't be so dismissive." She straightened. "I don't need a reason for you to be there. You're my niece and my apprentice. Nobody will question your presence."

I hoped she was right.

14

*F*lora and I were at the clinic bright and early the next morning. It looked like neither of us slept very well. Flora had taken on the role of overprotective aunt and was watching me like a hawk. I understood where she was coming from, but nothing was going to get me to sleep well last night. The fact that there seemed to be a curse targeting men in this town was disquieting, especially as there were several men that I was usually fond of.

Dr Collias met us at the front door. "Thank goodness you're here. We've had new patients come in and they're deteriorating fast. Nothing I'm doing is helping them. I can only hope you're able to provide the relief you gave the others yesterday."

"Have any woken up?" I couldn't help the hopeful note in my voice.

He shook his head. "No, but we've had no more deaths. That's a hopeful sign. Maybe this thing will run its course and the rest will be fine."

I wasn't so sure about that. I didn't think that we would

get through this without the curse tablet being destroyed, and that would only happen when the person who cast it was found.

"Where are the new patients?" Flora was all business.

"I have them split between two rooms." We followed the doctor to the hallway at the back of the clinic.

Flora made a big show of pulling out a small medicine bag and putting it in my hand. "Now remember what you need to do. This spell comes in two parts." She pointed behind me. "You do your part in that room and I'll do my part in this room, then we'll swap over."

I looked down at the medicine bag. Flora had made it up the night before, thinking that if I rubbed it over the patient's chest, it would hide the way I removed the tendrils. I walked into my allocated room and gasped with shock. Sitting next to a small crib containing a baby was Deputy Karl Iversen.

"What are you doing here?" I gasped.

Karl looked up and I could see redness around his eyes, stark against the mottled gray of his skin.

"My son, Reuben, took sick last night."

My knees weakened. It was one thing for this curse to target men, but now it was targeting children. I stepped over to the bed.

"What are you doing?" Karl asked, suspicion coloring his voice.

I hated lying to him, but his baby's life depended on me doing this.

"Yesterday we did a healing spell on some patients and it seems to stop the deterioration. It isn't a cure, but it gives us time to find one. Will you let me do this?"

Karl nodded, some hope in his eyes. I looked down in the crib and saw the telltale pile of black tendrils curled on the tiny chest. Anger streaked through me at the sight. If I needed any evidence that whoever did this was evil, I had it in this moment. I leaned over and, holding the small medicine bag in my hand, I wiped against the tendrils. I watched as they disintegrated when my skin came in contact with them. Some fell to the side and I tried to surreptitiously wipe them as well. Once I'd destroyed all of the tendrils that I could see, I wiped my hands up the baby's side, ensuring I had caught every piece of the curse.

"Flora will be coming in for the second part of the process." The part where we tried to hide what I had just done.

Karl stood up and pulled me into his arms. "Thank you."

"We're going to find out what this is," I whispered fervently before giving him a quick kiss on the cheek.

I pulled away and started working on the other three men in the room. By the time I was finished, Flora had stepped in and started her part of the drama. I gave her a quick nod when she caught my eye and crossed over into the other room. This room was bigger and held seven patients. As I started on the first one, Marigold walked in.

"What are you doing in here?"

I showed her the medicine bag. "Flora said that rubbing this on the welts would help."

"What's in it?"

I shrugged with what I hoped was the right amount of cluelessness and turned back to my work. "I have no idea. I'm just following orders."

I knew I had to be very careful. Karl had been distracted by his concern for his son so hadn't notice the weirdness of my movements. Marigold was clear-eyed, and she knew far more about magic than I did. She wouldn't be so easily fooled. I tried to limit my movements as much as I could, but in some cases that was impossible. She stayed watching me until Flora re-entered the room.

"Is there a problem in here?"

Marigold ducked her head in what I was learning was an act of submission in this town. It was interesting to see how hierarchy played out in Walker Bay. To me, Flora was the approachable aunt trying to protect me. To others she was an all-powerful witch.

"My apprentice is finishing the work I started. Are you questioning that?"

"Of course not. I'm sorry I interfered." Marigold ducked out of the room, but not before I saw a speculative look cross her features.

I continued my work in silence under Flora's watchful eye. After the last one I turned. "They're all done."

Marigold poked her head back in the room and I was a bit concerned that she had been hanging around the door. "We've just had another one turn up. He's still conscious. The doctor wants you to have a look at him."

THE EXAMINATION ROOM was a study in chaos. Violet Hally-bread and her daughter, Myra, seemed to be in a standoff with Dr Collias. Behind them stood the other two leaders of the Path Coven, Elspeth Pickering and Ilsa Hocking. The four women looked as if they were trying to intimidate the doctor. Magister Rigby showed every sign of being completely out of his depth as he stood to the corner next to an annoyed Magister Hartford. My breath caught as I realized who was lying on the examination table, his shirt open and a mass of tendrils squirming on his chest. Without a word I strode over to him. Despite my concern, I still retained my senses enough to keep the medicine bag in my hand as I pressed down on his chest.

"What are you doing?" Violet screeched as she reached for my arm.

Flora intercepted her, placing her back to mine. "We have been working on a healing spell for the patients. Not a cure, but it lessens the symptoms. We're hoping that applying it earlier will prevent him losing consciousness."

"I will not have your apprentice working on my son," Violet spat.

"If it makes you feel any better, I will be performing the second half of the spell."

From her response, I didn't think that Flora's offer was one she welcomed. Ignoring the women behind me, I focused on the task at hand. I glanced up and got caught by Julian watching me, pain flashing through his eyes.

"I knew you still cared."

"I've been helping Flora with this spell for the last two days. This doesn't make you special."

"Get away from my son, now!"

That wasn't going to happen. I lowered my head until my mouth was at his ear. "I need you to empty the room."

He looked at me quizzically.

"Just trust me, Julian. Please."

He nodded faintly. "I want everyone out, except Sadie."

"And Flora," I murmured as I held my hand tightly to his chest.

"Flora as well."

After much grumbling the room was cleared. I didn't miss the look Magister Hartford gave me. I could understand her enmity, but I didn't have the luxury of time to be delicate about her feelings. I didn't understand her relationship with Julian. She didn't seem to particularly care about him, but she was angry about the fact he'd been involved with me.

"Okay, Julian, I need you to lie back and close your eyes."

"Are you going to take advantage of me?" he murmured as he complied with my request. "I'm not saying I'm opposed. In fact, I think that might be just the thing to cure me."

I smiled. It would take a lot more than a curse to keep Julian Bernauer down. "You're not that lucky, my friend."

He sobered. "If this doesn't go the way we're hoping it will, I need you to know that I'm sorry."

I hesitated for a moment at the unexpected apology. "Thank you."

"I did care about you," he continued. "My father's family would never have approved me getting involved with a normal human. The situation with Penelope was set up when we were still babies. As far as everyone is concerned, it's a done deal."

"You don't have to explain."

I indicated to Flora to come over. Now that I had got rid of the tendrils on his chest, I could see the welts underneath. One thing I had noticed about the welts on everyone's chest was that they were all the exact same pattern. With Julian it was more intricate. Something made him different. I looked up to find him staring at me. Before I could stop myself, I reached a hand up and pushed some of his hair back.

"We're going to work out what this is."

"Should never have let you go," he mumbled, as his eyes fluttered shut.

"Don't close your eyes, Julian," I commanded.

He didn't respond. Flora stepped forward and shook his shoulders. There was no response.

I kept my eyes on his chest and watching it rise and fall was the only good part of this lousy day. "Looks like getting to them early doesn't make a bit of difference."

Flora did some movements with her hand above him. "He's just unconscious, exactly like all the others."

Flora went over to the door to let everyone back in.

I dipped my head and brushed my lips across his cheek. "Do not even think of giving up on me, Julian," I whispered harshly. "You already ran out on me once. You're not allowed to do it again."

My arm got yanked and I stumbled back. "What did you do to him?" Violet raised her hand and I was so stunned at what I knew was coming, I didn't even react. There was a deafening roar in the room. The next thing I knew everyone except Flora and I had dropped to the floor.

"You forget your place, Violet Hallybread." Flora's voice was strident and unforgiving. "Your coven exists at my indulgence. Do not abuse my generosity by laying a hand on my niece."

Violet whimpered, her hands over her head. Myra and Marigold cowered in the corner with Ilsa and Elspeth. I could see the two magisters trying to fight against Flora's power, but it was a losing battle.

As suddenly as it appeared the spell lifted, and Flora clasped her hands in front of her. "We need to work together to fight this affliction. That can't happen when false accusations are being flung around. The spell I have been using today is not a cure. It is merely a way to slow the pathway to death, to give us time to save the lives of the people we care for deeply."

Violet lowered her head. "I apologize Coven Leader. I was distraught at the thought of losing my son."

Flora nodded sternly. "I understand the love for family. My niece is everything I have, and I will protect her always."

I kept quiet, knowing the pronouncement she had just made was important.

"We will leave you with your son."

I didn't need her to tell me to go. I walked out the door without looking back.

As we made our way down the hallway, I glanced over at her. "I should be a lot more frightened of you than I am, shouldn't I."

Flora stopped and put her hand on my arm. "I never want you to fear me." She swallowed and glanced back at Julian's room. "What happened there had everything to do with me and nothing to do with you. Violet has been challenging me for years. Usually, I let it go, but I will not tolerate anyone hurting you."

We walked toward the front of the clinic in silence.

"Is he still conscious?" Dr Collias asked as he came towards us.

Flora took in a deep breath. "No, the spell seems to make no difference to that eventuality."

"Damn," breathed Collias. He scrubbed his hands against his face. "At least there haven't been any deaths today."

"How many did we lose?" I wasn't sure I wanted the answer.

"All together we have seven men who have died with those welts on their chest," he replied bleakly.

"Do we have any new cases, other than Julian?" Flora asked.

Collias shook his head. "No, usually I've been finding that they start coming in around the evening." He grasped Flora's hand. "I know you're frustrated that you haven't been able to break through this affliction, but you need to know that your spell is keeping these people alive. You have no idea how grateful I am."

Flora smiled faintly. "We'll be back tomorrow morning for any new patients," she said.

As we walked to the car, I couldn't help asking. "Why aren't we going back tonight if that is when most of the patients arrive."

Flora reached up and cupped my face. "You are exhausted. Situations like this have a tendency to gather speed. What we've seen so far is just the beginning. We need you to keep up your strength. I suggest you have something to eat and go to sleep." She looked away and I could see fear in her eyes. "I can guarantee that this is going to get much worse before it gets better."

*a*fter Flora dropped me off, I knew that I was never going to get to sleep with the sun so high in the sky, so I called Tilda and arranged to meet her at the diner. After all, Flora had suggested I eat something. Tilda was waiting for me when I got there.

I slid into the seat and looked up to find her watching me expectantly.

"What?" I asked slowly.

"You need to put out your troll doll."

I tilted my head, a little confused. "I thought my pathetic attempt was beneath the dignity of a proper witch."

"That's not what I said."

"Yet, that's what I heard."

Tilda rolled her eyes. "Will you put the doll out so we can talk."

I reached into my bag and put the doll in the middle of the table. "The cone of silence is now activated."

The waitress came to the table and took our order. For the first time I didn't get an accompanying sneer or glare. Usually, when I came into the diner, I always felt a layer of hostility, either from former girlfriends of the sheriff, or one of the werewolf clan who seemed to dislike me on principle. Today, there was nothing. A few furtive glances seemed to be the most that was happening.

"What's going on?"

Tilda looked around the diner and ducked her head to hide a smile. "Word is, Flora put a smackdown on the Path Coven."

I winced at her terminology. "I wouldn't call it a smackdown."

"I heard that it felt like they were being pressed into the ground by a giant rock."

I shrugged. "I wouldn't know, she didn't aim it at me." I tilted my head. "Anyway, how does that affect the way people are treating me?"

Tilda waited until the waitress had dropped off our order. "In reality, the Path Coven is only permitted to exist in Walker Bay because of Flora's good graces. The rules in most towns are that splinter groups are forced to find another area to practice. Flora chose to let the splinter group form when she became coven leader. Because of that, some people thought she was weak, and the Path Coven has been testing her patience for years. Some of them thought they could push her out, that she wasn't as strong as people thought she was."

"Is that what her coven thinks?" I wondered if that was why Isobel thought she could get away with cursing Flora.

"Nah, those of us who really know Flora, knew that nobody had found her line yet." Tilda put down her burger. "You, my friend, are that line. If anybody tries to come at you, there is not only going to be a berserker werewolf standing with you, but a witch who was considered so strong she became coven leader at the age of thirteen."

"You're saying that now people are too scared to treat me the way they've been treating me for the last few weeks."

"That's exactly what I'm saying."

"So, all that resentment and hostility is going to be pushed down, forced to fester in the darkness, and ready to explode when I least expect it."

Tilda grabbed a napkin and started to wipe her hands. "That's kind of a glass half empty way to look at things."

"I prefer to see it as being realistic." Wait a second. "How did you know what happened at the clinic?

Tilda waved her hand airily. "I heard it around. You know how gossip is in this town.

"No, your information is too specific to just come from gossip. I think you got this from somebody who was actually present. Violet, Myra, Ilsa, and Elspeth were there, but I don't think that they would be keen to talk to you."

I found it interesting that Tilda was refusing to look me in the eyes.

"Marigold was there, but I think she's too busy to contact you."

"Hmmm." Tilda was determined not to give away anything. Unfortunately, she had a fatal flaw.

"Of course, there was Magister Rigby."

And there it was. A flash of red stained Tilda's cheeks.

"Is there something you want to share with the group?"

Tilda finally looked me in the eyes, and I could tell she had wanted to share this information as it came out in a rush. "He's really nice. We talked for ages during my interview, and then he asked me out for dinner."

It sounded like she had a far better time at her interview than I did. "What exactly did he say happened at the clinic?"

"He called me straight after it happened because he's staying with Julian and had to cancel lunch. He said you and Flora were trying to help Julian and Violet tried to hit you.

He was stunned by Flora's power. It seems none of their files mentioned how strong she is."

I wasn't thrilled that Flora was now on the magister's radar. Come to think of it, I didn't know how I felt about Tilda's newfound relationship with a magister.

"You will be careful with him, won't you?"

Tilda looked confused.

"The magisters are only here for a short period of time for this investigation."

"Are you worried I'm going to get my heart broken?"

"I'm more thinking ripped out of your chest and stomped on, but I could just be remembering my own experience with a magister."

Tilda reached out and grasped my hand. "I like him. I really do, but I'll be careful."

"That's all I ask."

Tilda peered at me. "Are you okay? You look like you're about to fall asleep."

I stifled a yawn. All of a sudden, I felt like I'd been running a marathon. "I think I'd better get home. Flora told me earlier I should try to get some rest." I stood up and tucked my troll doll in my bag.

"Be careful," Tilda said, a worried expression on her face.

"Always," I replied.

I left the diner, fully aware of the eyes watching me go. I had a feeling this newfound atmosphere I was in was going to cause me problems.

One of those problems walked up to me in the street with rage flashing in her eyes.

"Magister Hartford, what can I do for you?"

"Stay away from him."

I really did not have the energy for this. "I am assisting Coven Leader Harstone. If you have a problem with my presence, you need to speak to her." I had to contain a smirk at the thought of Flora's response to this woman's demand.

"I don't care about his dalliance with you. We will be married."

I went to step around her and was stopped by a hand to my chest.

I couldn't help the smile as I looked up at her. "Are you sure this is the step you want to take?"

Her hand dropped as if it had been burned.

"What was between me and Julian is over. You don't have anything to worry about from me. I don't know how I can make that any clearer." I walked away, hoping that she'd got everything she needed by confronting me. I somehow doubted it.

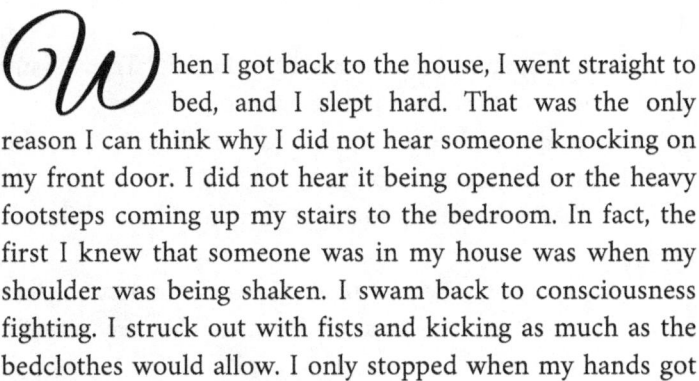

16

When I got back to the house, I went straight to bed, and I slept hard. That was the only reason I can think why I did not hear someone knocking on my front door. I did not hear it being opened or the heavy footsteps coming up my stairs to the bedroom. In fact, the first I knew that someone was in my house was when my shoulder was being shaken. I swam back to consciousness fighting. I struck out with fists and kicking as much as the bedclothes would allow. I only stopped when my hands got pinned and I heard a familiar voice.

"Sadie, will you stop fighting. I'm not going to hurt you."

I shook my head to get my hair out of my eyes. "Conall, what are you doing here?"

Conall lifted his hands away from my wrists. "I need help."

I pulled myself up into a seating position, clasping the bedclothes to me.

"What happened?"

"Eamon's come down with this illness. Collias said you'd been doing something to save their lives. He said you were coming back in the morning and that Eamon should last until then, but I need to do something now. I thought you could help him."

I could see the terror in Conall's eyes. Eamon was the only member of his family who had treated him well his whole life. I knew what it was like to face losing someone you love.

"I'll go with you," I said fervently.

"Others have died." He sounded broken.

I dropped the bedclothes and pulled him into a hug. "We're not going to let that happen to Eamon." I got out the bed and grabbed some clothes. "Now, I need you to go downstairs. I will be five minutes and then we will go to the clinic."

With a desperate look in his eyes, he left. True to my word we were out the door in five minutes.

We got in the sheriff's truck and Conall got us to the clinic in the shortest time possible.

Dr Collias was waiting for us at the front door. "Where's Flora?"

In my rush to help relieve Conall's anxiety, I had forgotten that I needed Flora for this ruse. This may actually work in my favor.

"I need you to go get Flora," I said urgently. "I'll get started on my part of the spell and she can finish off when she gets here."

"If you think that's best." I hated to see Conall like this. He looked so lost.

I followed Collias into yet another room. Eamon was lying on a bed, the wheezing sound as he struggled for breath told me that this was a worse case than the others. The massive clump of tendrils that seemed to engulf a good proportion of his body confirmed it.

"I need some privacy so I can concentrate," I said to the

doctor, hoping he wouldn't take it as a slight.

I was relieved when he complied with my request. It was going to take Conall a while to fetch Flora to the clinic. I needed to get as many of these tendrils off Eamon as I could before I ended up with an audience. I knew without a doubt that Conall would not leave his brother's side until he was convinced he wasn't going to die. I pulled off the sheet that covered him and started grabbing tendrils anywhere I could find them. Even with them disintegrating, there were so many and I was doing it so fast that a residue seemed to build up on my hands. Periodically I had to rub them together to remove the unpleasant feeling that seemed to cling to me.

By the time I heard Flora's voice in the hallway, I had removed and destroyed all the tendrils. I quickly grabbed the medicine bag and started rubbing it over Eamon's chest. I'd been moving so quickly and with such a focused determination that I hadn't stopped to check if his symptoms were calming down. I was relieved to find that his breathing was easier, and some color seemed to have come back into his face. Flora stepped up next to me and I stopped what I was doing and made room for her.

I watched, fascinated by the ritual she had come up with for her part of our ruse. As an outsider, I would think that it looked real. For all I knew, it was real and it was helping in some way. I could feel Conall vibrating with tension as he stood beside me. It felt natural for me to link my hand with his and try to will some of my strength into him.

When Flora was finished, Doctor Collias came over and started checking Eamon. "It was a good thing you came," he murmured. "For some reason he started deteriorating rapidly. I have no idea why."

I knew why. Something about this curse caused Eamon to get a triple helping. I had no doubt that if we'd waited until morning, he would have been dead, and Conall's heart would have been broken. I couldn't stop myself from squeezing his hand.

"He's doing better now. Heart rate back to normal, breathing is clear. I think what you're doing definitely helped."

That was a relief. I studied the welts that I'd uncovered on Eamon's skin. They covered his chest, arms and legs, and were far and away more intricate than any others I'd seen.

"Have any other patients come in tonight?" I asked.

"A few," Collias replied.

I looked over at Flora and caught her eye. "I think it might be a good idea for us to do the spell on them now, rather than waiting for tomorrow."

Flora nodded and we left Conall and Eamon as we went to check the others.

Fortunately, the other victims were nowhere near as complicated as Eamon. We were back to the standard clump of tendrils on the chest, and when I cleared them away, they had the same welts as everybody else. The most disheartening part was that we seemed to be getting more children. Young boys lying still on the beds when they should have been up and playing. It was heartbreaking to see.

While Flora was finishing up, I went to check on Julian. I was surprised to find him alone in his room. Between his fiancée, his mother and his sister, I had felt for sure that there would be somebody watching over him. As I drew closer to his bed, I was horrified to see the sheet moving. I pulled it back and found his body covered in tendrils. This wasn't supposed to happen. Without a thought, I started pulling at the squirming entities. It took a while, but I finally finished. I wasn't surprised to find the welts now covered his whole body. I felt, more than heard, Conall come into the room.

"I'd heard he was one of the afflicted."

What a terrible way to describe these people.

"Are you okay?"

I nodded, not trusting my voice.

Conall put his hand over my shoulder. I couldn't deal with sympathy right now.

"I need to talk to Flora," I croaked.

I ducked away from him and headed down the hallway, finding Flora as she left the last room.

I pulled her to the side. "We need to check everybody again," I muttered.

"Why?"

"I just looked in on Julian and he was covered in those things. He's now got welts all over his body."

"I don't understand."

Neither did I, but until I was sure not one tendril had survived, I was going to go over every single patient in the clinic.

A couple of hours later, I breathed a sigh of relief. Despite my fears, nobody else seemed to have been reinfected with the more virulent strain that Julian and Eamon had been attacked by. I'd even searched areas of the clinic to ensure the curse had not found some place to settle, only to attack patients when they were at their weakest. Flora had successfully managed to divert Doctor Collias, so I was able to move faster than I would have if I'd had somebody looking over my shoulder. The only concern came when I walked out of a supply closet to find Conall watching me keenly.

"What were you doing in there?"

I did not have the time or energy to face an interrogation. "Not that it's any of your business but I took a wrong turn, I've just been checking the patients that we've done the spell on to see if they needed further help and I'm tired. I just want to find Flora and go home to bed."

He caught my arm as I went to walk off. "Thank you."

I gave him a small smile. "It's not a cure, but hopefully it will give us some time to find out how to fix it."

Conall nodded grimly. He opened his mouth to say something else, but Flora interrupted him.

"Are you ready to go, Sadie?"

"Yes," I said gratefully. I was barely holding myself together. The last several days were catching up with me. I had never felt such bone-crushing fatigue and all I wanted to do was curl up in bed and sleep for days.

I let Flora lead me out of the clinic and bundle me in her car. The instant the engine started I fell asleep, my head leaning against the window. The next thing I knew Flora was pulling me out of the car and leading me into my house. She got me into my pajamas and tucked me in my bed as if I was a child. Even in my half dream state I could feel the worry she was trying to hide.

"We'll fix it," I whispered with a confidence that surprised me as I curled onto my side.

Flora dropped her head and gave me a soft kiss on the forehead. "I have no doubt we will, but I'm worried about the cost."

*T*he sun was high when I woke up. I felt better. I would have to remember getting more sleep when I was dealing with curses. It obviously depleted more of my energy than I was expecting. I quickly had a shower and threw on some clothes. I wanted to get to the library and do some more research. I knew that Isobel had hidden some books on curses around the library. I needed to make more of an effort to find them. The way the curse seemed to be attacking some patients in different ways concerned me. Flora and I had once discussed the possibility that curses were almost sentient. My worst fear was that somehow they could sense a cursebreaker and they mutated to make it more difficult for me to destroy them.

I was so caught up in my plans that I didn't even notice I wasn't alone in the house until I found Conall sitting at my kitchen table drinking coffee.

I noticed the tense way he was holding himself. "Is Eamon okay? Do we need to go back to the clinic?"

"Eamon's fine, or as good as he can be." Conall looked up

at me, his eyes seemed to be searching. "Were you ever planning on telling me you were a cursebreaker?"

My lungs seized as pure intense fear gripped me. "What are you talking about?"

Conall watched me sorrowfully. "I wish I could give you the time to trust me and feel you can tell me your secret. We don't have that luxury."

He put his coffee down and walked towards me. I took a step back and he stilled.

"I saw you last night when you were working on Eamon. That wasn't some healing spell. You were working on breaking the curse."

"But you were getting Flora." I was trying desperately to keep him from hearing the panic that was welling inside me.

Conall shook his head. "I called Flora and she drove herself to the clinic. I couldn't handle leaving Eamon."

I'd been so tired that I hadn't registered that Flora had driven me home in her own car.

I tried my last salvo. "Cursebreakers no longer exist. The families were all wiped out hundreds of years ago."

"And yet last night I saw you stopping a curse before it killed my brother."

"Why would you possibly think that? How did you make the leap from a standard healing spell to cursebreaker?"

Conall took another step towards me. "The Conclave isn't the only organization on the lookout for cursebreakers."

"Flora said…"

"Flora doesn't know what the Conclave has been doing. She has become so insular with protecting the coven here that she doesn't hear the rumors."

I put my hands over my eyes. "You need to leave. You're throwing around accusations that could get me killed."

Conall took the final step towards me and put his hands

on my shoulders. I know he could feel me trembling. He pulled me into his arms.

"I will never betray you," he whispered. "I will tear the Conclave apart before I let any of them touch you."

Flora's warnings were screaming loudly in my head.

"I don't know who I can trust," I whispered, praying that I wasn't making a mistake.

"Then I will tell you my secret," he replied simply. "Once you have that, you can decide what you want to trust me with."

He pulled me over to the couch and we sat down. He kept me in his arms, my head against his chest. It seemed easier for us to not be looking at each other while we were baring our souls.

"You already know that my life in Walker Bay was less than perfect. My father hated me and was pretty sure I wasn't his child. He let me know his feelings on a daily basis. Except for Eamon, my brothers felt that treating me like my father did was the way to go. My inability to shift made my life in the clan hell. If it wasn't for Eamon, I would have given up years ago."

"He sounds like a good brother," I whispered.

"He's an amazing brother, and one day he is going to make the best alpha that the clan has ever had." Conall's devotion to his brother came through with every word. "Eamon pretty much raised me from the moment our mother left. Nobody else was interested in the job." He sobered. "I know you keep hearing about the way I was in high school, and I will admit I was not a saint. Between the girls and my getting up to any trouble I could find, I think the town was glad to see the back of me when I left the day after graduation."

"What did you do?"

"I did what any boy with no family and no hope for the

future would do. I joined the military." Conall shrugged. "For the first time I found somewhere that didn't care that I couldn't change into a wolf. I was respected for my skills and I thrived. I figured I was going to be career military. Not because I had any great love for what I was doing, simply because it was the first place where I fit."

"So, what happened?"

I was recruited by the Assembly."

I frowned, trying to remember what I'd been told. "The Assembly governs all paranormals except witches."

"Despite what the Conclave would like you to believe, the Assembly has jurisdiction over them as well. Conclave law is usually a great deal stricter than Assembly law, so the Assembly allows the Conclave to have jurisdiction."

I frowned. "That doesn't sound very practical."

"It's been the way we've operated for hundreds of years. I'm not saying it's perfect, but it works. Kind of."

What did you do for the Assembly?"

I felt Conall's arms tighten around me. "I did what I'm good at, I hunted down those determined to hurt us and our way of life."

I could tell from the tension that vibrated through him that he was concerned I wasn't going to take that news well.

"And then what happened?"

"I came back to Walker Bay."

"Because you missed it?" Considering everything else he told me, that didn't sound right.

"Do you really think I would willingly come back to this town unless there was another reason?"

I had a bad feeling. "You're here to investigate something."

"A Seer came to us with a vision that there was going to be a cataclysmic event in the paranormal world, and ground zero was going to be here. For some reason she didn't feel safe enough to go to the Conclave with this prophecy, so she came to us."

"So, you're undercover?"

Conall nodded. "The Assembly has been concerned with the actions of the Conclave. Laws that have not been acted on in years are suddenly being enforced. The rhetoric coming from some high-ranking members of the Conclave indicates they want a return to the old days when the witches held dominion over all the other paranormals."

"How did you get elected sheriff? I would have thought the point of going undercover was to be discreet."

Conall grimaced. "That was not expected. I became a deputy as part of my cover, and when the last sheriff retired, I was put forward by the werewolf clan as their nominee for replacement. I've always thought Eamon had a hand in that. I can't see my father being too thrilled, but Eamon is his heir. That gives him some leeway when it comes to dealing with the alpha."

Conall took a deep breath in. "So that is my secret, that nobody in this town knows, except for you."

I guess that meant it was my turn.

"I broke the curse that had Flora imprisoned when I was first brought here. I didn't mean to do it. It just happened."

"I thought the coven broke the curse." Conall's voice was low, encouraging me to talk.

"According to Flora, there is no way the coven would be able to do that. It's how we knew that Isobel created the curse. She tried to fool the coven into believing they would be successful. She came back early that night, just after the curse had been broken." I closed my eyes as I remembered that time. "She tried to cast a second curse at Flora. The reason it backfired is because I stepped in front of her. It seems that the only benefit to this power is that I'm immune to curses and if one is thrown at me, it's like I'm a shield and it will ricochet back on the person who cast it."

"What is it you've been doing for everybody with this plague?"

"When I look at a patient, I see a clump of tendrils, like wriggling black snakes on their chests. When I touch them they disintegrate. I now need to find the tablet, or a manifestation of the tablet, and smash it. That seems to break the curse. Our theory is that destroying the tendrils weakens the tablet enough to allow me to destroy it."

"That sounds easy enough."

"Then I'm obviously not explaining it correctly. The last time I broke a curse I felt like something was screaming through my head and I ended up passing out."

Conall's body tensed. "This happened when you rescued Flora?"

"No, that curse was easy to break, that was the reason I was able to do it without even being aware I was a cursebreaker. Before she was murdered, Jeanette Hocking created a curse to protect that cottage that she was having the affair in. That was the one that kicked me in the head when I was destroying it."

"Flora was with you then, wasn't she?" Conall looked worried.

"Flora has been acting as my sidekick and mentor in this situation. She's always got my back."

I felt Conall's fingers running up and down my arms. "I've heard of cursebreakers, but I've only ever met one and that was in passing. I never got to talk to her."

My head shot up. "There are others? Did some of the families survive?"

An indescribable sadness crossed Conall's face. "No, the Conclave is nothing if not thorough. Every one of the cursebreaker families was wiped out."

"Then how…?"

"Nature is amazing, and sometimes it fills a gap. In the last few hundred years there have been several cursebreakers born spontaneously. The Assembly has been able to save two."

Those did not sound like great odds.

"What happened to the others?"

"They disappeared. It's assumed that the Conclave took care of them."

And the unrelenting terror returned. "Now that you know about me and I know about you, what do we do?"

"Now we need to focus on finding the person who released this curse on Walker Bay, and we get them to break it, or we find the tablet and work out a way for you to break the curse without anybody finding out." Conall spoke with the determination I knew so well.

I sat up, pulling away from him. "I'm assuming you have a plan."

"I'm going to deputize you."

I wasn't sure I liked that plan.

"You're going to what?"

"You're the only person who can see these things that indicate who is afflicted by this plague. You're the one person in this town capable of breaking the curse.

I nodded. "Those are logical points, but I don't have any law enforcement experience at all. I'm a librarian, for goodness sake. Isn't there training I need to do before you can deputize me?"

Conall ran his hand through his hair and I had to stop myself from smoothing down the bits that were sticking up. "Then you'll be a consultant. I don't have anybody on staff who knows as much about this as you do. I need you."

I could see a slight flaw in his plan. "You do remember that we have three magisters from the Conclave in this town.

If any of them was to get a whiff of an idea that I am a curse-breaker, my understanding is that my life expectancy will shorten considerably. Hiring me as your expert on curses is going to put a huge target on my back."

Conall looked at me sympathetically. "The work you've been doing at the clinic is going to put more of a target on your back. Are you willing to stop doing that?"

"I can't," I said hoarsely. "If I stop destroying those tendrils, people are going to start dying again. Some of them are children. Two days ago, I worked on Karl's newborn baby. I can't stop doing that."

Conall gripped my hand. "I know, and if I could see another way to solve this case, I would take it, but it has to be your decision. I will do everything I can to protect you, but I won't lie to you. You could be putting yourself at risk."

My mind raced as I went through all the possibilities that I could think of. The one thing I kept coming back to was that despite this so-called power of mine, I was barely making a difference. Sure, people weren't dying anymore, but they weren't living either. Julian proved that no matter what I did, I couldn't fix this until I found the person who cast the curse and destroyed the tablet.

"I'll do it," I said quickly before fear would make me change my mind. "Whatever you need me to do, I'll do it."

*F*irst thing that had to be done after my sudden career change was to inform my aunt. To say she wasn't happy was an understatement.

"Are you out of your mind?"

It hadn't taken long for Flora to get to my house after I called her with the news that I was Walker Bay's newest law enforcement recruit. Fortunately for me, she was saving her anger for the sheriff.

"She has no experience as a cop or a witch. You are making her a sitting duck."

"I would never risk her life."

I had to say I was impressed with the way Conall was holding his own against Flora. I had a feeling not many people in this town were willing to do that.

"And I can't believe you told him." Obviously, she'd decided I needed to feel a bit of her ire as well. "The last I heard you two were barely speaking to each other.

"This has nothing to do with our personal life," I insisted. "You know I'm the only person who can see when a curse has been laid. What if whoever has done this has laid other curses around town. We never believed that Jeanette wrote that curse that sent people insane, did we? Maybe whoever is doing this gave her that curse."

"And you just barely survived the experience."

"You might be exaggerating that a bit," I mumbled. "It was rough, but I don't think I was in danger of dying."

"You told me that it was trying to seduce you with power. You're new to this world and other than your curse breaking abilities we've had trouble getting in touch with your magic. Whoever is behind this curse is skilled in ways that are unimaginable. I'm afraid you don't have the strength to face them."

Ouch, that was harsh. I couldn't disagree with her, but it was still not pleasant to hear that my teacher had those kinds of concerns.

Conall stepped forward. "I won't let anything hurt her."

Flora snorted. "My understanding is that you already did that. How am I supposed to entrust the safety of my only family to someone who can't decide if he wants to follow a Destined Beloved prophecy?"

Okay that was a bit unfair. "I'm as much to blame for that mess as he is," I interrupted. "You can't hold him solely responsible."

Flora threw her hands in the air. "You two are just as bad as one another."

She pointed a finger at Conall. "I am holding you responsible for anything that happens to her, and I can guarantee that if she gets hurt you will not like what happens to you.

She turned and pointed that finger at me. "Do not do anything stupid that gets you killed, hurt, or exposed."

With that order ringing in our ears, she turned around and stalked out of the house.

"She's right," Conall said as he turned around to face me.

"We need to get the personal stuff out of the way before we can work effectively with each other.

Oh great, that was going to be a fabulous way to top off the day. I clasped my hands in front of me and sat primly on the edge of the couch. "Very well. Do you want to start?"

Conall began pacing. "That morning, I wasn't laughing at you. I was laughing at me. You're right. When I was younger, I jumped from bed to bed and it didn't mean a thing." He dropped to his knee in front of me. "Since the day I met you, I haven't been able to get you out of my mind. And remember, this was before the prophecy happened. All I knew was I had lived my whole life without a woman taking up any real estate in my brain, and all of a sudden, I found myself being distracted by you at every turn. When we were told about the Destined Beloved prophecy, everything clicked into place. In my mind, everything that has happened in my life had brought me to the point where I met you." He swallowed and looked away. "The reason I haven't taken the next step with you is not because I don't want to. It's because I want it too much. I know that you're it for me. I'm worried that you're not as sure, and I can't take the next step until I know that you are. I won't survive if you change your mind."

"I was hurt," I blurted out. "It felt like you thought that I wasn't good enough for you, and when you laughed it made every insecurity I had about this situation come screaming out. I feel like you've been forced into this situation. I mean, you've been with girls that are prettier, more outgoing, and more powerful than me." I swallowed nervously knowing that listing your faults to a guy was not particularly smart. "I'm not special and I'm just worried that the only thing tying you to me is the prophecy, and that one day you'll wake up and realize that this isn't what you want.

Conall chuckled. "So, what you're telling me is that we are both worried about the same thing."

I smiled tentatively back at him. "Looks like it."

He cupped my face. "I've told you before that I choose you." He looked away and I saw a flash of pain in his eyes. "I do think you need some time to deal with the Julian situation. You have unresolved issues there. I don't think we can move forward until you deal with them."

"You're right." I put my hand over his, enjoying for a moment the feel of it against my skin. Unfortunately, a moment was all we got. "We need for him to be conscious first," I said, adopting a business-like tone. "I agree we should start working on this investigation together."

Conall nodded. "You're right, but first..."

He leaned forward and kissed me. It was a kiss of passion, but also one of promise. I could feel his need in that kiss, and I couldn't stop myself from melting against him. I didn't even want to try.

Conall was the one who pulled away. "Remember that, any time you're doubting my feelings for you, remember that kiss."

19

*O*ur first stop was to meet Flora at the clinic. I needed to treat the new patients who had come in since we'd left earlier in the night. Fortunately, none of the new patients seemed to have been covered in the same way as Julian and Eamon. Having Conall watching my back while I plucked away at the tendrils gave me the ability to work quicker. We still kept up the charade of the healing spell, but I didn't feel like I was facing this situation alone. It was disheartening to see the number of men and boys now lying motionless with welts on them, marking them as victims of the curse. What was worse was there were now so many of them, the clinic was running out of room. I was finding makeshift beds in hallways and I couldn't help the anger I felt at the sight of a little boy looking like an angel except for the angry red welts on his chest, lying on a camping bed. As if he could read my mind Conall stepped forward and put his hand on my back, supporting me in the only way he could.

"We'll find out who did this," he whispered, his voice throbbing.

I nodded without speaking, knowing if I did I wouldn't be

able to contain my emotions. We left Flora to finish up the spell and headed for the Sheriff's office.

"You know how this is going to look, don't you?" I said nervously. "It's like you're giving your girlfriend a job."

"There's not much I can do about it," Conall sighed. "I need you. You're the most likely way I have of breaking this case."

"We just can't tell anybody that."

We pulled up out the front of the Sheriff's office and Conall turned to me. "Before we go in, I think there are a couple of things you need to be aware of. Most of these deputies are ones I have chosen myself. Historically, the Sheriff's department has been staffed primarily by were-wolves. I have brought in a larger number of the other races, and that means there is sometimes tension in the office. My father's enmity towards you may come through. Just ignore it as much as you can. If it becomes a problem, don't try to sort it out on your own. Come to me and I'll deal with it."

That sounded great.

"Second thing, don't ask Iversen about his family."

"Wouldn't that be considered rude?" I asked. "I was just in the hospital checking on his child. Shouldn't I ask Karl how he's doing?"

"That's the last thing you should do," Conall said patiently. "It's a cultural thing with ogres. They never talk about their families. I only found out his wife was pregnant by accident. It probably goes back to some time in history when ogres were hunted, but it's now so entrenched in their culture that nobody questions it. You can know an ogre all your life and have no idea about their family unit. It's just the way it is."

"Anything else I need to remember?"

"Any problems, you come straight to me."

"Yes, Sir." I saluted smartly.

Conall barked out a laugh. "I have a feeling there was sarcasm in that."

I smiled sweetly. "See, you are getting to know me."

To say that my introduction to the team had gone badly was a bit of an understatement. I'd had slightly interested looks when I walked in behind Conall. That had changed to outright hostility when Conall had announced quite bluntly that I was now part of the investigation team. In fact, it was the best way for me to tell who was a werewolf and who wasn't. Most of the werewolves were the ones who were glaring at me.

"She has no training or any right to be here at all." Hanlon's tone was seething with resentment. "I can't believe you're bringing her into the department. You would never do this if it wasn't for that prophecy."

It was obvious to everybody that the sheriff was barely holding onto his temper.

"Here's the thing, Detective Hanlon. You keep blaming everything on the Destined Beloved prophecy, but I would have chosen Sadie even without it."

I didn't know where to look so I chose to keep my eyes on Conall. He had just made a big statement in front of everybody and he didn't look embarrassed by it at all.

"Yes, the prophecy means I want to have Sadie with me at all times, but I would never allow it to interfere with the work we do. In this situation Sadie has information that we need. As some of you are aware, Flora Harstone and Sadie have been spending the last few days assisting those afflicted by this plague. Although they are unable to heal the victims, their efforts have meant that no more people have died. Apart from the medical staff, Sadie and Flora now have the most intimate knowledge of the symptoms of the illness. They have also noted differences in the way it has attacked various people. We are going to need that knowledge if we come across any more of the afflicted." He straightened his shoulders. "I'm not interested if you have an issue with this."

"May I have a word with you, Sheriff?" Hanlon asked through teeth that were gritted together so hard I was sure she was going to cause herself to have a headache.

"If you feel you must." Conall's voice sounded resigned.

I could see Hanlon wasn't the only one with a problem. However, because she was a liaison from the state police and the only one that didn't come under Conall's direct control, she was the only one who could disagree with impunity. Or so she thought.

Conall pointed me towards a chair as he followed Hanlon into his office.

"This is going to be fun," a voice cackled behind me.

I looked around and found a dwarf sitting at the desk beside me. "You're Deputy Beastpike, aren't you? I don't think we were properly introduced the last time we met." I remembered him doing forensics on my house when Brian Tolan had painted a warning on the side of it with blood.

"Just call me Pike. Most people do."

"I'm Sadie."

"Oh, I know who you are. You'd be hard-pressed to find anyone who doesn't know you." He nodded his head at Conall's office door. "Don't worry about that. She's going to rant and rave and threaten to call somebody who she thinks has power, but really doesn't. In the end she'll storm out of here and go running to the alpha. The alpha will then come in here and try throwing some dominance about which won't work on the sheriff."

"You've seen this act before?" I queried.

"Many times. That woman may think she's all that, but she is a lousy cop."

I winced as I noticed the inordinate amount of interest

shown by some of the werewolves. "You might want to keep those opinions to yourself."

Pike looked around. "Everyone knows my opinion of the dominance hierarchy. It's not going to come as any surprise."

"I'd just prefer not to have a bigger target on my back than I already do."

Pike grinned. "Bit late for that. They still blame you for their precious Brian Tolan being in prison."

"Because it's my fault he kidnapped me and tried to kill me," I muttered.

"Blind loyalty makes people stupid." He paused. "You might want to start carrying something for protection."

"You mean a gun?" I didn't like the sound of that. I knew how to shoot a gun. My mom had been a single mother working two jobs and living in a not very nice area. She'd got a gun for our protection and made sure that I knew how to use it. I could see the attraction in having that level of protection. I still wasn't fond of them.

"I'd suggest a stun gun. Works far better."

I had to admit I was surprised. "You prefer to use a stun gun?"

Pike nodded. "And pepper spray. We don't use guns around here very much. Despite all the theories regarding silver bullets, killing a werewolf is really hard to do." He winked and gave me a smile that was just this side of chilling. "But causing them pain is surprisingly easy."

I jumped when the door to Conall's office was flung open and Hanlon stalked out. She didn't look at anyone as she made her way out of the office.

"Told ya," murmured Pike.

"Anybody else want to take a personal day?" Conall asked, barely holding onto his temper.

Nobody made a sound.

"Sadie," he barked. "In here."

Oh, we were going to have words about that.

I followed him into the office and waited until he had closed a door. I put up my hand before he had a chance to speak. "I recognize that you are having an emotional day so I am not going to make a big issue out of it now, but I'm just letting you know that if you ever order me around like that again we are going to have a massive argument."

To his credit, Conall looked a little shamefaced. "I'm really sorry about that. It won't happen again."

Slightly mollified, I took a seat.

Conall cleared his throat. "I don't know much about curses, so I need you to fill me in on everything you know."

"You want to talk about it here?" I was aghast at the cavalier way he was dealing with my secret. There were at least three werewolves out there who would have no problem taking this conversation back to their alpha. The same alpha who would be only too happy to pass the information on to the Conclave.

Conall put up his hands in a placating gesture. "This office was warded by Flora. Nobody can hear a word that goes on in here, and it can't be bugged."

I nodded, slightly appeased by his explanation. "From my experience a curse requires a witch sacrificing part of her soul and carving the curse on a stone tablet. From there, these black tendrils seem to be created. In this case the tendrils settle in a knot on the victim's chest. Except for Julian and Eamon. With them the tendrils pretty much covered their entire body."

"Conall looked thoughtful. "Do you have any idea why that would be."

I shrugged my shoulders. "I don't know. Maybe because they're powerful. Julian is a magister and the son of a Conclave member and a coven leader. Eamon is the son of the alpha and the most likely successor to your father. That could be why it hit them harder."

"Do all curses have a curse tablet?"

I shook my head. "I found one that was written on paper under the bed in the cottage that Jeanette was using for her affairs with your father and brother. That one seemed to be about making somebody love you so much they became a kind of slave."

Conall closed his eyes and shuddered. "If the clan found out that a witch had cast an enslavement curse against an alpha and his son, there would be blood in the streets. What happened to it?"

I frowned, wondering whether he would be happy or not with my explanation. "I set it on fire. It was so terrible that I couldn't let it survive. It seemed to be looking for another witch to use it. I sometimes wonder if these things are alive."

"And because you can't tell anybody that you're a curse-breaker, nobody knew it even existed." Conall shook his head. "I can't believe Jeanette did something so stupid. If anybody found out, Brian would have grounds to defend the murder charge."

My mouth dropped open. "What do you mean? He killed her. We both know that."

"A witch using their abilities to enslave anyone is considered provocation. If it came out that Brian fought against the enslavement curse and killed her in the process, the court is more likely to give him a medal than convict him."

"And what about what he did to me?"

Conall shrugged. "The curse could be considered mitigating circumstances and you were collateral damage."

It was going to take me a little time to get my head around the intricacies of paranormal law, but for now we had other problems. "I don't know whether it was Jeanette that created the curses. I mean, she cast them, but they didn't feel like she created them." I grimaced. "Maybe I'm not explaining this properly."

"You think another witch could actually be creating these curses and passing them on to other people to cast." Conall dragged his hand through his hair. "Well, that's just great." He sighed. "Are there any other forms a curse tablet could take?"

"Flora mentioned that some in the past had used human skin and it seems that a cursebreaker can use their own body to cast a curse. They don't need to create a physical medium."

I squirmed a bit in my seat at Conall's speculative gaze.

"Could it be another cursebreaker?"

"I don't know. According to Flora, it was a group of cursebreakers who created the Black Death plague in the Middle Ages. This seems to be something similar."

Conall started pacing across the office. "Except this one only seems to be targeting men in Walker Bay."

"Is there anything linking these men?"

Conall stopped. "What do you mean?"

"Well, this is a pretty major curse so I would suggest we're looking for a tablet. Carving out a tablet is a laborious job. It's not like you would choose specific names because that would take forever. It has to be a subset of men." Something was starting to move in the back of my mind. "I mean, why has Eamon come down with it and not you? With all due respect, I would have thought if people were targeting specific men in this town, you would have been front and center."

Conall grinned wryly. "Nice opinion you have of me."

I rolled my eyes. "You know what I mean. You're a threat to anyone who is trying to do something wrong in this town. If somebody wanted to get away with this, taking you out of the picture is the best way to go about it. We already saw that in the way your father used Hanlon when Jeanette was murdered."

Conall grabbed a piece of paper off his desk. "This is the latest list of victims that Collias has sent through. Maybe we can find something linking these men."

I looked at the sheet. "I don't know any of these people except Julian and Eamon."

"Then let's focus on those two."

I closed my eyes as I tried to concentrate. "One's a werewolf and one's a witch. They're both the sons of leaders."

"Aidan's got five sons," Conall reminded me. "Only one of them is sick."

"The eldest one," I mused. A thought struck me. "Julian's the eldest son too."

Both of us froze and Conall snatched back the paper, his eyes racing through the names. "They're all firstborn sons."

"That's why it's getting children as well. If the curse was made to attack firstborn sons, it wouldn't discriminate about their age." Another thought rolled through my head. "What about your father? He's the alpha. Wouldn't that make him a firstborn son?"

Conall shook his head as he continued to go through the list. "Aidan defeated his older brother for the role of alpha."

A horrible thought hit me. "Are there many firstborn sons that aren't on the list?"

Conall raised his head. "Hundreds of them."

I gripped my hands together. "So, either it is just a coincidence that those that have been hit so far are firstborn sons."

"Or we're only at the beginning, and the worst is yet to come." Conall's words echoed in the room as we both contemplated the horror that Walker Bay could now be facing.

20

"*W*here is he?" A voice roared outside the office.

"Oh, for the love of...can't I get through one day when I don't have to deal with this?"

Looked like Pike had been right and Hanlon had gone running to the alpha.

I followed Conall out of the office to find a rampaging werewolf in the main area.

"Office, now," Conall barked.

Aidan looked like he was going to argue but then reconsidered his options. He didn't exactly look meek about it, but then I doubted he ever could.

"Would you like to join us, Sadie?"

I got a wink of approval from Pike. I wasn't sure how I felt about that. I followed the two men back into Conall's office. I could understand why Conall would prefer this conversation in a soundproof room, but with two testosterone laden werewolves in a small area, I was beginning to feel a little claustrophobic.

"How dare you bring that woman into an investigation?" Aidan spat.

"Last night that woman helped save Eamon's life. I would suggest you treat her with some respect." Conall leaned forward against his desk, the menace obvious in his tense body. "Not to mention, there's a side of me that takes it very badly if I think there's a threat to her."

For an instant I saw fear in Aidan's eyes. I knew he disliked his son, now I knew he feared him. That was a dangerous combination. I saw him squelch the fear down and draw himself taller.

"She has no place in this investigation."

"I say she does, and frankly, my opinion is the only one that counts. If your pet doesn't like that she is more than welcome to go back to the state police."

I winced. It seemed that even verbal fights between werewolves had no rules.

"Despite how disappointing you've been as a son, I didn't think you would stoop so low as to be a witch's lapdog," Aidan sneered.

I was afraid that was going to set the fur flying until I saw Conall's smile. "I'm not a werewolf remember, you cast me out. I'm part of the coven. Your prejudices don't apply to me anymore, not that I would have listened to you anyway." Conall pinned Aidan with his gaze. "Now I am going to make something very clear to you. Despite what may have happened in previous administrations, while I am sheriff you have no say in this department. Do not come back trying to throw your weight around because I will shoot you down every time out of principle. This department is no longer owned by the werewolf clan. Everyone in this town will be treated equally, no matter where they lay on the hierarchy or which clan they belong to."

The longer Conall spoke, the redder Aidan's face got.

"You will regret this, boy," he snapped as he stormed out of the office.

I closed the door after him and watched as Conall dropped in his chair. "Are you okay?"

Conall sighed, the exhaustion from a sleepless night evident in his voice. "I sometimes wonder why the last sheriff put me forward for this job. I'm beginning to think he was tired of the control Aidan had over the department and knew putting me in here was going to mess things up for him." He looked up at me. "This was not part of the original plan when I came back here."

"I'm sure it wasn't, but personally I'm glad you're the one in that seat rather than another one of your father's lackeys."

Conall's eyes were drawn back to the list. "I like the first-born theory, but it would be a mistake to assume we're right."

Unfortunately, I had to agree with him.

He reached over and passed me a large file that had been sitting on his desk. "This is the information we have on every victim of this thing. I know you're not a cop, but you've got more knowledge about how curses work than the rest of us. Maybe something will leap out at you that we would have missed."

I wasn't very hopeful, but at this stage I was willing to try anything, so I nodded sharply.

Conall smiled, his appreciation obvious. "I'll organize a desk for you here."

For the rest of the morning I went through the files. I learned more about my neighbors than I really wanted to know. I compared the information from those who died to those who survived to see whether there was more at work than my abilities. After several hours of work, I had come up with precisely zero. I leaned backward in my chair, my head tilted, and my hands over my eyes.

"I'm guessing you're not having fun," drawled Pike.

"How do you do this day in and day out?"

Pike chuckled. "I get my jollies where I can."

I glanced around the room and noted that I still seemed to be the center of attention. "Is that ever going to stop." I didn't bother to lower my voice as the werewolves would be able to hear what I said, no matter how quietly I whispered.

"The niece of the coven leader with the son of the alpha. According to the werewolf clan there are so many things wrong with that pairing, they don't even know where to start."

I could hear low growls coming from some of the werewolves. I wasn't sure if they were aimed at me or Pike. At that moment I didn't care. As I'd glanced around the room my eyes had landed on Deputy Greensmith. He'd done a truth reading on me once at a crime scene and we belonged to the same coven. I barely knew the man but, in that moment, I knew we had another problem. I stood up suddenly and strode purposefully into Conall's office. I could tell I was supposed to knock before entering by the irritated expression on his face as he looked up. That changed when he got a look at me.

"What is it?"

"Greensmith is sick. I saw tendrils moving under his shirt."

Conall frowned in confusion. "He looked fine."

"He's not fine," I whispered. "We need to get him to the clinic. I don't know how long it takes from the first time the tendrils show to coma, but I don't think we have a lot of time."

Conall pulled open the door. "Greensmith, get in here."

Oh great, now he was going to think I was complaining about him. We were going to have to talk about Conall's communication skills.

Jim Greensmith was usually a nice-looking guy with the most beautiful golden hair I had ever seen on a man. Unfortunately, I couldn't get past the tendrils that were crawling all over his body, as if they were looking for a place to settle.

Conall looked over at me expectantly. It seemed I was the one who had to handle this.

I smiled tentatively. "Jim, how are you feeling?"

He shrugged. "I'm fine."

"Have you been having any flu-like symptoms?"

"I'm fine," he said, a little bit louder.

As I watched, a tendril slipped from behind his ear, leaving a welt that snaked down his throat. I glanced over at Conall and could see that, even though he couldn't see the tendrils, he could see what they left behind.

"I think you need to get to the clinic. I've been working with some of the patients and I can see the early stages. Flora may be able to help you." I figured any mention of the coven leader was going to work in my favor.

Jim's eyes widened and he took a step towards me, and then stopped as he seemed to waver. Conall and I both reached for him as he began to collapse. We each grabbed an arm and started dragging the deputy to the main office.

"Pike, we need help," Conall growled.

The small man leapt up, grabbing keys. "Not Jim."

I nodded wordlessly as I tried not to cringe at the tendrils that were making their way around his body. One thing I was grateful to see was that the second the tendrils touched Conall they backed away as if they couldn't go any further.

We loaded the deputy in the truck and held on while Conall got us to the clinic as quickly as he possibly could.

I stayed in the back with an increasingly agitated Jim Greensmith. "What's happening?" he muttered.

"We're getting you to the clinic," I soothed as I discreetly tried to dislodge as many of the tendrils as I could. I felt like I was fighting a losing battle. It seemed that Jim had received a dose of the super curse, and the sheer number of tendrils was more than I could cope with in the back of a car. I took a moment to send a text to Flora. I knew I was going to need her.

We screeched to a halt in front of the clinic. Conall and Pike jumped out and helped me unload a now unconscious Jim Greensmith.

I was surprised to find Flora already waiting for us at the door. "You got here quick. I just sent the message."

Flora smiled grimly. "I've been here all day, trying some different spells to see if they make a difference."

"Did they?" I asked, unable to keep the hope out of my voice.

Flora shook her head. "Nothing I do is helping."

I read the subtext. If we couldn't find the curse tablet or the person who cast this curse, there were no other options.

"I think Jim's got a bad case," I said, hoping she was understanding what I was telling her.

Flora nodded sharply and indicated where we should take him. She led me to a back area that looked suspiciously like it used to be a storage room, and we put Jim down on the makeshift bed.

I glanced at Conall and, understanding my meaning, he barked at Pike. "Watch the door and make sure nobody comes in here."

When the door was closed, I turned to Flora. "I need to remove the tendrils from his entire body, not just his chest.

Flora nodded sharply and started undoing Jim's clothing. As she worked, I went about destroying the tendrils. Conall took a step back and watched as the two of us treated the deputy quickly and efficiently. It was a sad state of affairs that we had become so adept at our tasks. We moved quicker when we heard loud voices outside the room.

"Have you got them all?" Flora asked urgently.

I scanned Jim's body and nodded as I ran my hands up his sides to ensure no tendrils were hidden.

Flora nodded to Conall and we pulled a sheet up to cover the man as Marigold pushed her way in.

"What are you doing?" she cried as she raced to the deputy's side. You could see that she desperately wanted to touch him, but felt it wasn't her place.

I raised an eyebrow at Flora, and she nodded. Looked like the young healer had a thing for the deputy. I wondered if he knew.

Flora stepped over to Marigold and put an arm around her. "We were just doing some spells on him as early as possible."

"Why can't you fix this?" Marigold cried, her eyes seeking mine.

I didn't know how to respond. The worst part was, I was the only person who could fix this. I just didn't know where to start looking. My only resource was books. There was nobody I could talk to who had an intimate knowledge of curses. My throat went dry as I realized that there might be somebody I could talk to. I looked over at Flora who was comforting the distraught younger woman. I had a feeling the hardest part was going to be convincing my aunt to let me try.

I left Flora and Conall to talk to Marigold and went outside to join Pike. I was surprised to find him talking to Liam Rigby.

Pike beamed. "Here's the newest member of our department. Nice work picking up on Jim being sick."

Liam looked confused. "I thought you were a librarian. I wouldn't have imagined that assisting with investigations was one of your normal duties."

Pike snorted. "She's part of a Destined Beloved prophecy. Normal doesn't come into it."

"And you've been able to help with this plague?"

"Yes, Magister Rigby," I felt wary at the seemingly inno-cent question. "Flora has been working on spells to try to cure the plague. She came up with one that needs the two of us to work on it. Unfortunately, it's only managed to slow down the progression. Nothing we've done has managed to stop it."

"Please call me Liam," the magister said with a sparkle in his eye that gave him a boyish look. I could see why Tilda was so enamored.

"We're doing the best we can, and if there's a way to stop this plague, we'll find it."

"I hope so," he said. "Julian's a good friend. I can't believe he wasn't able to fight off this infection."

"How's he going?" I asked, trying to keep a casual tone in my voice.

"Same as before," Liam replied. "I was just going to see him now. Did you want to come as well?"

I shook my head. "I don't think that's a great idea," I said warily. It was one thing for me to see Julian when I needed to help him medically. It was completely different if I was to be just a visitor.

"I understand," Liam said thoughtfully. "Hopefully I'll see you later."

I gave him a quick nod. If he spent any more time with Tilda, I could almost guarantee it.

After he left, Flora and Conall came out. "Is she going to be okay?" I asked, concerned about the young healer.

"She'll be fine as soon as Jim wakes up," Flora said, tension radiating from her body.

"Has anybody contacted his mother?" I asked, confused by the look shared by Flora and Conall at my straightfor-ward question.

"Elspeth Pickering isn't a part of her son's life anymore,"

Flora said gently. "She gave up all parental rights to him when he was fourteen. It's the way of their coven."

"And I can guarantee that Jim doesn't want her here," Conall added.

That thought made me unbelievably sad. "Violet is showing concern for her son," I pointed out. "Maybe Elspeth will be the same."

"You're forgetting Magister Bernauer's status. Violet believes that a bit of maternal concern now and then will benefit her." Flora looked as though that statement was distasteful. I didn't blame her.

"Are you ready to go back to the office?" Conall asked.

"Actually, I was hoping to go to the library. I had an idea and I just wanted to do some research on it before putting it forward as an option."

Conall smiled. "I'll drop you off on the way to work and then pick you up in a few hours."

I nodded. That sounded fine. Flora was looking at me in a way that said she knew I was up to something but wasn't sure what it was. I wasn't ready to fill her in before I could see whether my idea was as bad as I thought it would be.

$\mathcal{O}$nce Conall and Pike had dropped me off at the library, I went to work. Before long, I had a number of manuscripts in front of me and spent the next few hours looking for any small piece of information that would indicate that my plan had a chance of working.

My research would have gone faster except I kept being interrupted by people coming in and out of the library. It seemed I wasn't the only worried witch searching desperately for a way to stop this plague. Everyone seemed to have their own ideas on what needed to be done to cure it, and they'd come to the one place they could get information.

Since I'd become librarian the rules governing who could enter the coven library had eased but there were still some rules which could not be broken. Unlike a normal library, the books couldn't be removed from the building. If somebody wanted information they needed to come in, look for it, and then meticulously copy the information that they wanted. Some of the younger members of the coven had taken to using their phones to photograph the pages they were interested in. The older coven members were horrified by this break with tradition and dismissed it as the younger generation becoming lazy. They'd also shot down my suggestion of cataloging every book on a computer system. That didn't stop me from creating a simple database that was for my personal use. I also used it to help people when they came in looking for a specific item. Slowly, it was gaining a following. Once I'd persuaded enough members of the coven to the value of a computerized system, I would try again.

I stretched my arms above my head, trying to get rid of the kinks that had developed from the position I had been working in. I was becoming frustrated. I knew what I wanted to do. I knew it would help us get information about this curse. I just needed to find how to do it safely, or else Flora would never support me in trying it. Unfortunately, I didn't think I'd be able to do it without her help. I slammed shut the last book in disgust and went hunting for more information.

To say I was surprised to find Elspeth Pickering and Ilsa Hocking requesting entrance to the library was an understatement. Despite the fact the library was for the Walker Bay Coven, there had never been any rules preventing members of the Path Coven from coming in and looking for information. My understanding was that Flora hoped small gestures like this would lead to a warmer relationship between the covens. As far as I could see, it hadn't worked, but Flora lived in hope.

I approached the two women. "Can I help you?"

Elspeth and Ilsa paused for a moment as if surprised at my question.

"We've been coming here for decades," Elspeth sniffed, her tone exuding disdain. "I doubt we need your assistance."

I kept a smile on my face. "If you need anything, please feel free to ask." My duties as librarian discharged, I went back to dealing with my own problem.

I was up on the rolling ladder, trying to reach a book on

the top shelf when I heard a voice below me. "Can you please pass me the Hadren manuscript."

I looked down to see Elspeth peering up at me, a slightly annoyed look on her face. I reached over for the manuscript and started stepping down the ladder. "Is this the one you were looking for?" I asked as I handed it over.

She grunted as she started looking through the papers.

"You know Jim's come down with this plague. He's at the clinic at the moment." The words were out before I could stop them. It was one of those moments when you know you're making a mistake, but you can't seem to stop yourself.

Elspeth scorched me with a look of pure fury, tossed the manuscript papers on a nearby desk and stormed off.

I rubbed the heel of my hand against my forehead. "That was so stupid," I muttered to myself, unable to believe that I thought she'd want that information.

"You're wasting your time," Ilsa said.

I gasped at the silent approach of the woman dressed in black. "What do you mean?"

"Elspeth disowned Jim Greensmith when he was fourteen years old. She did that because she truly believes in the right-eousness of our cause."

"How righteous could a cause be that means a mother has to lose her child."

A shadow passed over Ilsa's face and I could have kicked myself for forgetting that she had only lost her daughter recently.

She put her hand up before I could apologize. "I under-stand what you're saying, and it is difficult for outsiders to comprehend why we believe what we believe. I would suggest you respect our beliefs and stop pushing your values onto us."

Before I could reply, she turned around and headed out the door. Nice, I'd managed to alienate both of the coven leaders. I'm sure Flora would be thrilled with my efforts. I shrugged. There wasn't much else I could do, I'd already opened my big mouth. I climbed up the ladder again. I remembered a book I'd found while cataloging for my computer system. It didn't deal with curses specifically but talked about other planes of consciousness. I knew there was a possibility that I was reaching for an answer that wasn't there, but I was starting to get desperate. I needed to find that curse tablet and destroy it. We had no other options.

After looking through several books I finally found what I wanted. I sat on the top rung of the ladder and started reading.

"That does not look comfortable."

I jumped at the sound of Conall's voice and grabbed the bookshelf behind me before I fell. He secured the ladder as it wobbled.

"Please come down before you kill yourself." He sounded polite, but I could hear the exasperated tone in his voice.

Gripping the book I had been reading tightly to my chest, I carefully made my way down the ladder.

"What are you doing here?"

"I'm taking you home, remember?"

I couldn't believe the day had gone so fast. "I'm not finished yet, but I think I'm close to an idea. I just need a little more time. You get going and I'll find a ride home when I'm done."

Conall looked at me sourly. "I'm driving you home today. I am perfectly capable of keeping myself entertained until you're finished."

"Good." I had already focused back on what I had been reading. I could feel that I was close.

I settled myself at a table and started taking notes. In a move that I knew would outrage traditionalists in the coven, I also took photos of pages to ensure that I got not just the words, but an accurate representation of the diagrams that went with them.

Two hours later, I thought I had enough to convince Flora that my idea wasn't just the best course of action for us to take. It was also the only one.

22

"*A*re you completely insane?"

I had a feeling that Flora would not look particu-larly favorably on my idea, so I was prepared for that response.

After Conall and I had left the library we had met up with a frustrated Flora at the clinic. In what had become a macabre routine, I removed the tendrils from the new patients and checked the previous patients for any signs of re-infection. While I concentrated on the afflicted, Flora and Conall ensured that nobody could see what I was doing. I breathed a sigh of relief to find that no new patients had the super strain of the curse. By the time I had finished I was starting to feel that familiar fatigue. I could see the worried expressions on Flora's and Conall's faces.

I knew my assurances that I was fine didn't help much but I needed them to focus on the situation, not me. Anyway, the knowledge that I had an idea that could help was giving me a bit of energy that the hopelessness of the situation had been sucking out of me. Conall had offered to get us some food for dinner, and this meant that I had some time with Flora to outline my plan. It was not going well.

I held out my hands in a stopping motion. "Just listen to my idea before you shoot it down."

Flora sat down on the couch with a mutinous expression on her face.

I proceeded to pace in front of her. "I've been doing some reading. I thought it was you who pulled me to your side when you were under the curse that Isobel cast, but I'm beginning to think that it was me who had the power to do it. Is that correct?"

"My magic was bound so it's unlikely that it was me." That admission seemed to be torn from Flora.

"If that is the case, do you think it would be possible for me to do the same thing with Isobel?"

Flora jumped up and started pacing as well. "You want to jump into the middle of a curse and interview the woman who tried to kill both of us."

I wouldn't call it the best plan I'd ever had but I couldn't see any other options. "There are babies and children who are going to die from this disease." I pleaded with her to understand. "These curses started with Isobel. If anyone can give us a hint why this is happening or even who is doing this, she is the one."

Flora shook her head forcefully. "No, I will never allow you to do something so reckless."

Before I could argue a deeper voice joined the conversation. "I have no idea what you're talking about, but I agree with Flora."

I closed my eyes as frustration washed over me. I had at least hoped to have convinced Flora of the rightness of my plan before tackling Conall. Unfortunately, it looked like I was going to have to take them both on at the same time. I straightened my shoulders and turned to face the sheriff.

"When Flora was cursed, I would visit her while I slept. I thought she was pulling me into the curse, but after the research I've done, I now think that I was the one controlling my communication with her."

Conall didn't speak. He just watched me with those pale blue eyes of his.

"Isobel is currently in a very similar curse to the one she put Flora into. Theoretically, it should be possible for me to communicate with Isobel." I kept speaking quickly to prevent Conall from interrupting with the objections I knew he would have. "Isobel is the one person available who knows about curses. Even if she doesn't know who cast this curse, she may be able to shed some light on how it was done or where the curse tablet is most likely hidden." I looked beseechingly at Flora. "I wouldn't even suggest this as an option unless I truly felt that it was our best chance of finding out who did this."

"I don't like it," muttered Conall. "Isobel is where she is because she tried to cast a curse at you. She'll be angry and bitter. We don't know how dangerous she could be in that state."

I glanced over at Flora. "You said that your magic didn't work when you were trapped. Isn't it a safe bet that Isobel is the same?"

Flora nodded slowly. "She could still be a danger to you in ways that we don't know. Isobel was one of the best of us. I can guarantee that she will have spent the last couple of months working on getting out of the trap she created."

I could see that neither of them would entertain the idea of doing this, so they were leaving me with no choice. "I'm not asking for your permission. I'm asking for your help."

I could tell they were both surprised at my statement. I had delivered it calmly, without any anger. I knew that I was dealing with two people who were used to being in charge and expected people to simply acquiesce to their demands. If I was going to have decent relationships with them, they were going to have to learn that I was not one of the people they could order around.

They reacted in completely different ways. Flora dropped on the couch, a stunned expression on her face, and Conall stalked out the front door.

"I should have expected the Harstone stubbornness to rear its ugly head."

I gave Flora a small smile. "My mother always said it was the Goodwin strong will."

Flora rubbed her hands over her face. "Do you at least understand why we're so scared of the thought of you doing this?"

I knelt down in front of her and grasped her hands in mine. "I'm not particularly keen to talk to Isobel, but if we don't find out who's doing this, people are going to start dying again." I turned away as I could feel tears burning my eyes. "I can't let Karl's baby die when I could have done something to save him."

Flora pulled her hand from mine and cupped my face. "I know you worry about being a cursebreaker. I know the thought of the power seducing you terrifies you. This is why I have confidence in your ability to resist it." She sighed. "I'll help you with your plan."

"I think you're both insane," Conall growled from the doorway.

I pulled myself to my feet, ready to face the next argument. "Do you have any idea who did this?" I asked quietly.

"You know I don't."

"Then I don't see that we have any choice. She may not be able or willing to help us at all, but I can't face another day of pulling darkness from the bodies of our friends and neighbors or their children, knowing that there was something that I could do but was too afraid to try it."

I could see Conall understood my argument, but he was fighting with his primal instinct which was to protect me from any form of danger. The moment he lost the argument with himself he pulled me into his arms.

"You're going to be the death of me, you know that, don't you?"

Considering the number of times he'd had to come to my rescue, I certainly hoped not.

23

*I*t had been decided that the best way for me to prepare for going into Isobel's curse was to get some rest. That was easier said than done, but I eventually fell into a deep sleep. It seemed the exhaustion in my body was able to trump the restlessness in my mind. When I woke up, I was surprised to find Flora downstairs doing the last thing I expected.

"You made me breakfast?"

Flora passed me a plate covered in pancakes. "Eat up. You're going to need your strength today."

I enthusiastically covered the pancakes in maple syrup and tucked in. "These are good."

Flora smiled and added some bacon to my plate.

"Do you have any more of that?"

I looked up and found Conall in the doorway. "What are you doing here?"

"I may not be able to go into Isobel's curse with you, but I am going to make damn sure nobody touches your body while you're gone."

Some tension went out of me knowing that even though

Conall vehemently disagreed with what I was doing, he'd support my decision. "Thank you."

Conall grabbed a seat and accepted a plate from Flora. "I still think you're crazy to do this," he said darkly.

So close to perfection, and yet so far. "I know," I said simply.

"So, how are we going to do this?" he asked, his gaze sweeping from Flora to me.

"When Flora was cursed, it happened while I was asleep. I didn't seem to have any power over it. I'm guessing it happened automatically because you were family." I hopped up and grabbed my notes and phone, ignoring Flora's sniff of disdain when I showed her the pictures of the pages I felt were important. "I think this spell will simulate that situation and allow me to direct where I'm going."

"How do you get back?" Conall asked, obviously preoccupied with the one part he was most invested in.

"Because I am directing where I'm going, I can choose to return at any time."

"And if something goes wrong and you can't get back?"

And I thought I was pessimistic.

"That's why Flora will be doing the spell instead of me, other than the obvious lack of skill on my part. As the spell caster she will be able to wrench me back if I get stuck. It won't be pretty, but it will be effective."

Conall nodded as if he was satisfied with that answer. We continued to eat in silence as Flora studied the spell.

"It looks simple enough. I have the ingredients for the sleeping draught at my house. After breakfast we'll go back there and start setting up." She looked at me carefully. "We'll go to the clinic after you've done this. I don't want you facing Isobel when your strength has been depleted."

I could see the logic of that statement, but I still felt a

certain amount of guilt at the risk we were possibly taking with somebody else's life.

She must have seen my concern at that statement and her expression softened. "I'll call Collias and check to make sure we don't have any of the serious patients," Flora relented.

I smiled weakly. "Thank you."

Flora dusted her hands off with a flourish. "In that case, I will head home and start gathering everything together. You two finish here and come over when you're ready."

After gathering up my notes and taking my phone she left, leaving me to deal with a tense berserker.

"You need to stop doing this," Conall muttered darkly.

"Doing what?"

"Risking your life."

"You do it every day," I pointed out.

"I'm a cop," he stated as if that answered everything.

"And I'm a librarian."

Conall raised an eyebrow and I could see his point. Usually librarians weren't considered to have a high-risk occupation.

"I'm the coven librarian," I amended as if that made a difference. Considering some of the spells I'd come across while working, it probably did.

He raised his hand and cupped my face. "Promise me that if things get hairy at all you will come out of it immediately."

"I will," I replied softly. "I'm not looking to be a hero. I'm just hoping for a clue that will help us."

Conall's eyes searched mine and he nodded sharply. "We'd better get going then. The sooner we start, the sooner this day is over and I can start breathing again."

I smiled apologetically. I hated to be the cause of so much worry for him.

WHEN WE PULLED up at Flora's house, I was surprised to see Violet Hallybread knocking on her door.

"What do you think she wants?" I asked Conall.

"Nothing good, I'd warrant," he replied, his voice tight with tension.

I hoped Violet wasn't going to be difficult because I had a feeling that Conall was quite willing to take his stress out on anybody who kindly presented themselves.

Flora opened the door as we walked up and stepped out on the porch, closing her front door behind her. I saw Violet's features tighten at the slight Flora had given by not inviting her in the house.

"What do you want, Violet?"

I winced. It looked like Flora was not in the mood to be diplomatic today.

"I want to know what you have been doing to my son," Violet replied. "He is not getting any better. I need to know what you have been using so I can improve upon it and cure him."

I drew in a breath at the sheer arrogance of the woman.

"It's an old family spell," Flora replied shortly.

"You need to give it to me," she snapped. She looked at me with a sly expression. "My son's fiancée is troubled by the amount of time your apprentice is spending with him. It is unseemly how she is fawning over him."

Flora raised an eyebrow. It was quite amazing how much could be conveyed by that slight movement. In this case, it was informing Violet that she was close to getting tossed off the porch.

"No." Flora turned, dismissing Violet and walked back into the house.

Not knowing what else to do, Conall and I followed her. Once the door was closed, there was silence as if Violet was deciding what she should do next. It didn't take long before we heard angry footsteps as she walked back to her car.

"This way," Flora said sharply.

By this point I think both Conall and I were too wary of Flora's mood to do anything but obey every word.

My stomach dropped as we followed her into the basement. I knew that for witches the basement was where they did most of their spell casting. I also knew that as part of my apprenticeship to Flora I was going to have to set up my own basement for that very reason. I was not looking forward to that day. My one and only visit to the basement in my house had given me nightmares, not to mention a twisted ankle when one of the steps gave way. I had no idea how I was going to turn it into a place I could feel comfortable in.

As we descended the steps into the basement my nervousness eased. I wouldn't call it bright and airy, but it also didn't make me think horror show. Right up until I saw an open area surrounded by symbols. "What's that?" I croaked, pointing at the circle with candles flickering around the edges, that looked a little too much like a sacrifice was about to be made. I only felt a little better when Conall sought out my hand and squeezed it tightly. Seemed I wasn't the only one getting the creeps from this whole setup.

"It's a spell circle," Flora explained patiently. "Surely you've seen one before."

Now that I thought about it, I had seen one before. Of course, the one I'd seen before had a murdered witch in the center of it, and the symbols had been there to ensure the destruction of her soul. In fact, the person who did that murder was Isobel, the witch I was about to spend some quality time with. Wasn't that a pleasant thought?

I let go of Conall's hand and stepped forward. "What do I need to do?"

Flora picked up a large cup filled with a liquid which looked a little too much like a health drink for my peace of mind and pointed to the floor. "You need to lie in the center of the circle and drink this. It will send you to sleep but still allow you enough lucidity to guide yourself in your sleep state."

I eyed the cup hesitantly as I took in her instructions. "Any hints about what I should do from there to ensure I get the right person."

"What were your thoughts before falling asleep when you visited me?" she queried.

"I was worried about you," I said bluntly. "Just knowing that we could be family made me want to help you even more. I'm not having those same feelings in this situation."

Flora shrugged helplessly. "I don't know how to advise you. I would suggest that you concentrate on the Isobel you knew, even though it was for just a short time."

I straightened my shoulders. I could do this. More importantly, I had to do this. "I'm ready."

Before I entered the circle, Conall stopped me with a hand on my arm. He turned me around and kissed me sweetly. When he pulled back, he rested his forehead against mine and looked deeply into my eyes.

"I am going to be here the whole time. You need to come back to me so I can continue with my plan to charm you into accepting my courtship."

I smiled at the sentiment. "Don't worry, I've got too many things to do with my life to take any stupid risks."

I pulled away from him and gave my aunt a hug. I then grabbed the goblet and stepped into the middle of the circle. Knowing that the concoction Flora had made would send me to sleep pretty rapidly, I sat on the floor before downing the potion in one swift gulp. I grimaced. Yes, that tasted just as revolting as I thought it would. I tossed the cup at Conall and lay down on my back on what I was hoping was a newly cleaned floor.

"How long should this take before I go out?" I asked as I closed my eyes.

"It should be very soon," Flora replied soothingly. "Just focus on where you want to go."

I centered all my thoughts on speaking to Isobel which was a lot harder than you'd think. It gradually got harder and harder to hold that focus until I felt myself drifting and darkness took hold.

24

The last time I'd done this I'd gone to sleep and then magically found myself in a tower with my terrified aunt, imagining I was having a dream. Naturally, things didn't go quite so easy for me this time. Instead of finding myself in the tower, I found myself back in Flora's basement, except I was floating above my body. Seemed that foul concoction she gave me allowed me a little more control than I was prepared for. Rather than let myself become distracted by how freaked out I was by the similarity to a near death experience, I allowed my eyes to drift closed and forced every thought to focus on Isobel.

I felt a rush of air against my skin and the next thing I knew I was standing back in the dark, miserable tower that I had hoped never to see again. I glanced around the small room and saw a dark lump huddled in the corner.

"Isobel?" I ventured, careful not to make any sudden movements.

The shadow started to move, and I held my breath as she shuffled into the moonlight. The time she had spent trapped in her body showed. Her gray hair was no longer in the meticulous bun it used to be in. It was dark and matted and her clothes seemed to hang on her. It was hard to reconcile that this whole situation was just a manifestation of her mind and not an actual place. I looked around the room and tried not to flinch when I saw the curse tablet she had created embedded in the wall, the familiar black tendrils crawling around it. I wondered if Isobel could see it. I wasn't willing to ask in case it gave her a clue to my real abilities.

"How did you get here?" she croaked, her voice seemingly raspy from lack of use.

"Not entirely sure," I replied warily. "Flora and I were trying to contact you and it seems to have worked."

A cackle filled the air. "And why would the great Flora Harstone want to speak to me?"

"A curse has been laid in Walker Bay. It's an illness affecting firstborn sons. They get chills, muscle aches, headaches and then they go into a coma and nothing we do seems to wake them up. They're also covered in welts, some worse than others."

Isobel gave a hacking cough. "And you're coming to me for advice."

"You're the only person we know still alive that has cast a curse," I said simply.

"So, I'm your resident expert."

I shrugged helplessly. "You're the only chance we have. When I say firstborn sons, it isn't just men. There are children and babies being struck down with this thing. We need help and we don't have many options." Flora kept insisting that Isobel had been a good person once. I was hoping that she was right and that I would be able to reach the woman she had been before ambition took hold.

My hopes sank when I saw the cunning look in her eyes. "What do I get if I help you?"

"What do you think we can give you?" I asked warily.

Isobel struck her hand against the wall. "I want out of here," she demanded.

"You cast the curse," I whispered. "Aren't you supposed to be able to break it yourself? I thought that was the only way curses could be broken." I tried to put as much sincerity into my voice as I could.

Isobel hit the wall again. "Don't you think I've tried? I've done everything I can think of to get out of here. Nothing works."

"Why not?" I couldn't keep the genuine interest out of my voice. In the days following Isobel's curse backfiring, I had been terrified that she would break out of her prison and come after us. When that didn't happen, I was relieved. I was also perplexed.

"I think there was something built into the curse that stops me from getting out."

"Why would you do that?" I asked, the confusion evident in my voice.

"I didn't do it," she snapped.

"But…" I stopped as what she was saying filtered through. "You didn't craft the curse on your own. You were working with somebody else."

"You're smarter than I gave you credit for."

"Who was it?" I asked urgently.

When she just stared at me, I grew frustrated. "Whoever this person was, they're leaving you in this hellhole. They haven't tried to rescue you, have they?"

Isobel dropped her head. "I wasn't willing to sacrifice enough."

She sounded like she deserved to be in here, and not for the reasons that a normal person would. She deserved it because she hadn't been evil enough. My mind flashed back to the mangled body of Helen Napier, the woman Isobel had sacrificed for the curse against Flora and nausea hit me. "Was it worth it?" I croaked. "You lost everything, all in a quest for power. You had friends, family and a position of respect, and you threw it away. Tell me who convinced you to do that."

"No," she said simply.

"Why not?" I demanded, shaking as I restrained my anger.

Isobel lifted her head to gaze at the moonlight, a serene expression on her face. "Because the day is coming when our people are going to claim their rightful place in this world. We are not meant to scurry like rats in the shadows." She looked at me keenly. "While I've been in here, I've had time to think."

Great. The unhinged witch had been thinking. What could possibly go wrong with that?

"I think that you are more than you appear."

I stayed silent, knowing that if I disagreed with her too quickly, she would take that as confirmation.

"I think you could be swayed to our cause."

"No," I said simply. "I don't want to be a part of anything that hurts innocent people."

Isobel sniffed at me. "So high and mighty. It's easy to be like that when you don't know any better." She looked at me keenly. "But you will soon."

I suppressed the shiver that coursed through me. That sounded like a threat. "Do you really think that a return to curses is the way to go?" I demanded. "Put that kind of power back into the general population and you may as well give them missiles. Do you think only the righteous would wield that kind of weapon? They'll be used for petty, stupid issues by the most vindictive of us. Good people won't want to play with dark magic." I couldn't believe that she couldn't see that.

Isobel smiled. "We just need the right leader."

I snorted. "And you thought that was you?"

She ducked her head. "I would never presume. I was to be a servant at the right hand."

"Of who?" I growled, surprising myself at my impression of a certain berserker werewolf.

"The prophecy tells all," she nodded sagely, and I could see by the expression on her face that she was losing her grip on reality.

"It obviously doesn't tell all or you wouldn't be trapped in here." I knew I had limited time and Isobel was leading me around by the nose. "It looks like you weren't good enough for the prophecy. You failed." I knew I was being cruel but nothing else seemed to be working.

Isobel dropped to her knees as if the strength had gone out of her. I hardened my heart and resisted the urge to help her up. This was not the time for compassion. She started muttering and I had to take a couple of steps closer to hear her.

"There is always a purpose and an offering. Without the offering there will always be a flaw. I should have made more of a sacrifice. I just couldn't." She looked up at me and her face was ravaged with grief. All of a sudden everything became clear to me. Why she was trapped here. Why this new curse was so much more powerful.

"Margot should have been your sacrifice, but you couldn't do that to your twin."

Fear shone in her eyes as she realized she'd said too much. "You don't know what you're talking about."

"That's why you're stuck in here. To truly cast the curse, you should have included Margot as final proof of your loyalty to the dark magic, but you couldn't because she was innocent." I leaned forward. "There is good still in you. Margot is suffering without you. If I could tell her that you helped us find who did this curse, that may go some way to alleviate the pain she is feeling."

I thought I was getting through, I truly did, right up until the point she launched herself at me, her hands bent into claws. I barely caught her wrists in time before her fingers scratched my face. Fortunately, she was a lot weaker physically than me, because I would never have been able to fend off her manic struggles if she'd had even a little more strength in her body. I held her out away from me as she flailed wildly.

"Isobel, you need to tell me who is creating these curses. Help me save the people of Walker Bay."

Suddenly she stopped moving and I let go as she slumped against the ground. She looked up at me and, despite the exhaustion in her countenance, there was a fiery hatred in her eyes.

"Let them all burn."

I looked down at the bitter woman with anger and pity. She'd given me something and I hoped it was enough, because I knew we were never going to get anything else from her. As the rush of air hit my skin, I hoped that the information I had was enough to stop the curse. My last thought before the darkness took me was about the devastation Conall would feel if he lost his brother.

25

To say I was shocked when I opened my eyes and did not find myself back in Flora's basement was an understatement. The room I did find myself in was white and clinical. There were no windows and no door. All it had was what looked like a hospital bed with a figure lying on it, covered by a sheet. Ignoring everything in me that screamed that I should be concentrating on getting home, I took a couple of steps towards the bed and sucked in a breath when I realized who I was looking at.

I shook the shoulder gently. "Eamon, I need to speak to you."

When all I got was an annoyed grunt, I shook him again. "Eamon, I need you to wake up."

A seductive smile crossed the sleeping man's face. "Tilda?"

Okay, that I was not expecting. His hand snaked up behind the nape of my neck and he pulled my head down towards him. In a panic, I slapped a free hand over his mouth.

His eyes snapped open, and the look of horror on his face would have been funny if it wasn't quite so insulting. He scrambled back quicker than I would have thought a man of his size would have been able to. He pulled the sheet up to cover himself and looked for all the world like a medieval virgin on her wedding night. Despite the seriousness of the situation, I had to fight to stop myself from laughing.

"What are you doing here?" His voice was a little high and panicked. "Please tell me I'm not having one of those dreams about my brother's Destined Beloved."

"Calm down," I said dryly. "You're currently under some kind of spell which has affected a lot of the males in town. At this moment you are unconscious in the clinic.

"Thank goodness," he breathed. "Wait a second, if that's the case, what are you doing here?"

"Flora and I have been trying to work out what's going on. I was sent in to get some information from the victims."

Eamon's lip curled at the description of himself as a victim.

I looked quickly around the room and, unlike Isobel's tower, I did not find a manifestation of a curse tablet or the tendrils. That meant this curse was different. I should have known things weren't going to be easy. I focused back on Eamon.

"Is there anybody in particular that you have upset lately, most likely a witch?"

Eamon shook his head slowly. "I generally have a pretty good relationship with witches."

I wrinkled my nose at why a werewolf would say he had a good relationship with witches.

Seeing my expression, Eamon hurried to correct me. "Not the way you're thinking. I'm the alpha's firstborn son, I'm required on occasion to fulfill the parts of his position that he may not have time to do. To do that effectively I have to communicate with a wide range of people in town. I generally try to keep on everybody's good side."

I must have looked skeptical because Eamon sighed.

"I'm not my father. I know he has his faults, but I am not like him."

He sounded defensive, and I knew it wasn't fair to judge him on the alpha's behavior. From what Conall told me, Eamon had picked up the parenting duties when their mother left, and his father decided he wasn't interested in the defective son. For that alone he had my gratitude. I was hesitant to ask my next question, knowing that it would be a touchy subject, but it needed to be asked.

"When I first arrived, you thought I was Tilda and tried to kiss me. Is there something going on there that could be a reason for you being targeted?"

"The eldest son of the werewolf alpha could never have feelings for a witch." Eamon's expression was bitter as he spat the words out.

"But you do have them, don't you?" I asked quietly.

Eamon hesitated, as if unwilling to give voice to his innermost secret. He hung his head. "For a very long time."

"Have you told her?" I asked gently.

"How can I?" he growled. "It's not like I can do anything about it."

I wish I could disagree with him, but I knew he was right. If Aidan Tolan was furious because his disinherited son was involved with a witch, he would be apoplectic if the heir apparent did the same thing.

"I'm sorry," I whispered, and I really was. Both Tilda and Eamon were good people, but old prejudices were going to stop them from even having a chance.

Eamon closed his eyes. "Do you know why this is happening?"

"Not yet, but I think we're getting close to working it out." I tried to give him an encouraging smile. "Whatever you do, don't give up. I don't know what's coming down, but I need you to fight as hard as you can to get back to us. Can you do that?"

Eamon nodded. "If it doesn't work out the way we're hoping it will, I need you to tell Conall that I'm proud to have him as my brother and I love him."

I could feel tears welling in my eyes. Conall was right. Eamon was pretty special. He was the one facing losing his life, but his main concern was his little brother.

I stepped back to give us both some room. "I'm going now, but just remember we are going to get you out of this, you just need to not give up.

I closed my eyes and concentrated. The rush of air went through me and, when I opened them, I found myself in another white room, this time with Jim Greensmith lying on the hospital bed. I smiled to myself, pleased that I was getting the hang of this.

"Jim," I called softly, deciding after the last experience I would try a hands-off approach with dealing with these men.

He sat up with a start, ready to do battle, when he noticed me in the corner. "What are you doing here?" He looked around. "Where am I?"

"You came down with the illness that's been going through town. Flora sent me to talk to you to see if there was a reason you were specifically targeted."

Jim contemplated that for a moment. I'd hoped mentioning his coven leader might make him more willing to talk to me.

"I just do my job. Being a deputy always makes enemies, but one ready to take down half the town? I'm not that important. They'd be going after the sheriff, not me."

Just what I wanted to hear. I cringed at the thought of bringing up a touchy subject.

"How about your mother?"

Jim's face turned to stone. "We don't even acknowledge

each other exists. She wouldn't even notice if this thing killed me."

"I'm sorry," I whispered, hating the hurt he tried to hide.

Jim rubbed his hand over his face. "Look, I'm with the Walker Bay Coven. If this is a targeted spell, then they've screwed up by including me. I'm not that important."

I nodded. "Okay, thanks for your help. We're doing everything we can to get you out of this. We just need you to keep fighting as much as you can.

Jim nodded as I stepped back. "Thank you for not giving up on us."

I looked at the weary man and made a decision to poke my nose where it really didn't belong. In my defense, Eamon's hopeless feelings for Tilda played a part in my next actions.

"Marigold Syms was devastated when you were brought in," I said softly.

Jim's eyes flared with hope, but it died down just as quickly. "She's a good healer, she cares about everybody."

I put a hand on his arm. "Jim, I've been working next to her for days. She is kind, compassionate and dedicated. What she does not do is fall apart at the sight of every patient she knows. When I say she was devastated that you were brought in, I mean she reacted in a way I've never seen her react before. You might want to think about that when you get out of here.

"I'm a discarded kid whose own mother didn't want him. What do I have to offer someone like her?"

I shrugged. "I don't know. I just think that you making a decision for her is not fair. If you feel anything for her, I would suggest you talk to her, find out what she feels before dismissing it as impossible."

He nodded cautiously, but I could see the hope back in his eyes.

"Good luck," I whispered before focusing on my next stop.

I barely felt the air this time, the transition was so smooth. Unlike with the last two men, Julian was not asleep, he was prowling around the room, pushing on the walls as if looking for some way of escape. He had his back to me, so I spoke quietly in the hope of not startling him.

"Julian."

He whipped around, but rather than bombarding me with questions like Eamon and Jim, a wolfish smile spread across his face. "This situation has just started looking up."

"We need to…"

I didn't get a chance to say another word because he strode up to me and grabbed my face before heading in for a kiss. In shock I dropped my chin and managed to bang his face with my forehead before he made contact. He dropped his hands and we both stepped back.

"What the…?" he grunted.

I put one hand to my aching forehead and one hand out in front of me, palm up. "I believe I already told you that I didn't want you kissing me."

"This is a dream, isn't it?" he muttered. "I'm sure I've had this dream before." He peered at me, still holding his nose. "Course, last time I had this dream, you were wearing something a little different."

I rolled my eyes. "Seriously, Julian, this is not the time."

"Not a lot else to do," he muttered as he pulled his hand away from his nose and checked it for blood. Not finding any he leaned back against the hospital bed and crossed his arms. "If you're not part of my dream you might want to explain what you're doing in my head."

Happy to be back on safe ground I put my hand down. "You're currently in a coma from the illness you came down with. We now have about a hundred victims and they all seem to be firstborn sons."

"That can't be a coincidence," Julian muttered as I watched him go into magister mode. "Sounds more like a curse."

"That's one of our theories." It shouldn't have surprised me that Julian made the leap to the truth.

He looked at me keenly. "So, what's being done?"

"The coven is trying several healing spells with varying levels of success. The good news is we haven't had any more deaths since we started treating the patients."

"We just end up in a vegetative state," Julian said with a trace of bitterness.

"Unfortunately, yes, but everyone is trying to work out who did this." I took in a deep breath. "I need to know if there is anyone who you think would do this to you, specifically."

Julian eyed me keenly. "Why me? I'm sure you have dozens of options. Why do you think this curse is aimed at me?"

"We're not sure," I confessed. "It's just there are three of you who have welts on your bodies that are far more severe than the others. I'm just wondering what makes you so special?"

"Oh, honey," he said in a seductive voice. "You already know what makes me special."

"Will you stop doing that and concentrate on what's important," I demanded angrily.

"If you don't think what we had together is important than you seriously misunderstood how I felt about you."

I decided ignoring him was the best way to go. "I need to know why you three were targeted."

Julian shrugged. "I'm a magister. I have numerous enemies who would like nothing better than to do something like this to me. I don't see them taking out half a town to do it though."

"I think you're underestimating your effect on some people," I muttered.

Julian smiled as if I'd told him a joke. "So, who are the other serious cases?"

"Eamon Tolan and Jim Greensmith," I replied.

Julian contemplated my answer. "So, the firstborn sons of the werewolf alpha and two of the leaders of the Path Coven. I guess that makes a kind of sense. The witches and the werewolves are the strongest groups in Walker Bay. If you wanted to destabilize the town, it would be the way to start."

I began thinking about it. "If they were targeting the leadership of the witches and werewolves, wouldn't Flora and Ilsa have been targeted as well?" I asked.

"If you think about it, they already have. Flora was the victim of a curse and Ilsa's daughter was murdered. To an outsider, the leadership of Walker Bay looks like it's under attack."

And we had another theory to add to the mix. I rubbed my hand over my face. "I need to get back and talk to the others."

"Why were you the one the coven sent into this curse to talk to me?"

Why did he have to ask so many questions? "When Flora was under her curse, she managed to pull me in to talk to her. We decided to see if it would work again. My body is currently lying on the floor in her basement in the middle of a spell circle."

Julian grinned. "You've come a long way in a couple of months, haven't you?" He sobered suddenly. "Did you miss me at all when I left, or did you just get on with your life?"

"I really don't have time to get into this." I stepped back, ready to send myself back to Flora's basement.

Julian moved fast and grasped my arm. "Please, I need to know what you feel for me, whether you can move past what happened."

I was furious that he was pushing this conversation. Why couldn't he just leave the past where it belonged?

"You left me," I gritted out. "You want to know if I was devastated that you left? Fine, I was. I couldn't believe that somebody I had cared so much for could treat me so badly, especially after I'd told you I loved you. But if you think I feel the same way about you now, you are seriously deluded. Conall is my Destined Beloved, and nothing you say is going to change that, because he is more than just a prophecy. He is a good man who will stand by me no matter what anybody says or does. He has proved time and time again that I am the only one for him. If it wasn't for my stupid insecurities, we'd probably be married by now." I froze as what I'd said hit me square in the face. I was the only reason we weren't fully together. Conall was waiting patiently for me to catch up. Man, I owed him an apology.

Julian took a step towards me. "You will never understand how sorry I am that I didn't fight for us," he said quietly. "Leaving you was the hardest thing I have ever done and I regretted it immediately. If there was some way to go back and change things, I would."

"What's done is done," I said. "Right now, the only thing I'm interested in is finding the person who caused this plague and forcing them to destroy it." I stepped away from Julian and closed my eyes. "Just keep fighting, we'll get you out of this."

26

I half expected to find myself floating on the ceiling again, looking down at myself, which I'm the first to say was all kinds of creepy. Instead, the first sensation I had was unbelievable pain throughout my entire body, followed by an argument that seemed to be happening above me.

"You either get someone here that can bring her back, or I am taking her to the clinic myself."

I winced at the sound of Conall's demand.

"You are not touching her. We move her too soon and there could be serious consequences." Flora sounded like she'd gone into mama bear mode.

"What are you two arguing about?" I croaked as I struggled to get my eyes open.

"Finally."

I watched as Conall broke the spell circle, which I knew from Flora's endless lessons was a big no-no. I tried to sit up but gasped in pain as my whole back seemed to spasm.

"Don't move," Conall said authoritatively. "Flora's getting some heat packs that might help."

I tried to breathe through the pain. It didn't work. After what seemed like hours, Flora came down the stairs with a couple of heat packs and a small bottle. Conall pulled me into a sitting position and looked tortured when he saw tears of pain falling from the corners of my eyes.

"I'm so sorry," he whispered.

Flora placed one of the packs against my lower back and shoved the bottle at me. "Drink this," she said urgently.

At this stage I wasn't in any condition to argue, so I instantly swallowed the contents of the bottle. I felt a warmth flow through me and slowly the intense pain began to subside to a dull throb.

I groaned with relief. "What was that?"

"That was the result of lying on a solid concrete floor and not moving for over four hours," Conall replied.

I frowned at his statement. "Four hours? That doesn't seem right." If I had to guess I would have thought I was gone for less than an hour.

"We need to get you away from here," Conall said as he leaned down and picked me up as if I weighed nothing.

He started up the stairs with Flora behind us. After getting me settled on a couch with the heat packs working their magic on my abused back, the two looked at me expectantly.

"Did it work?" Flora asked.

"In some ways yes, in some ways no. Yes, I got to see Isobel and let me tell you she has not seen the error of her ways."

"What do you mean?" asked Conall.

"Well, in our discussion she ranted about some prophecy, she's angry she is stuck where she is, refused to tell me who helped her with the curse or who is the leader of some movement she wants to be a part of. She then tried recruiting me for the cause, and then she attacked me."

Conall frowned. "Did she hurt you?"

"No, surprisingly I was able to hold off the crazy lady who is old enough to be my grandmother."

Flora leaned back in the chair as if deflated. "So, it was a waste of time."

I shook my head. "I wouldn't say that. She let slip one little piece of information. She said that the reason her curse failed is because she didn't make enough of a sacrifice. It seems the most powerful curses need both a purpose and an offering. The offering needs to be important enough to match the curse."

"What does that mean?" Conall looked confused but I could see the dawning look of understanding on Flora's face.

"Her sacrifice should have been Margot," she whispered, the horror in her voice evident. "How could I not see that she had fallen so far?"

"An offering and a purpose." I could almost see Conall's mind working. "We have three victims who are completely different to the rest. At least one of them has to be the purpose and one of them is the sacrifice."

"I also spoke to Julian and he thinks that Walker Bay itself is being targeted. Flora was hit by a curse, Ilsa Hocking lost her daughter, and now Aidan, Violet and Elspeth are all in danger of losing their sons. That's a fair number of the more powerful people in the town."

"You spoke to Julian?" It looked like Conall had focused on only one part of what I said. "Exactly how and why did you do that?"

"When I was just about to leave Isobel, I had a stray thought about Eamon. Next thing I knew, I was in a room with him fast asleep on a bed. I woke him up and we talked about whether there was any possibility of someone targeting him. After that, I figured if I could speak to Eamon, maybe I could speak to the others. I next jumped to Jim

Greensmith and then to Julian. I just thought that interviewing the victims was something we should do if we had a chance."

Flora looked perplexed.

"What?" I asked.

"Being able to jump from one person's unconscious mind to another. That isn't something most people can do. I just don't understand why you seem to have so many problems with basic spells, but you can easily accomplish feats that the most powerful witches would have trouble with."

If she didn't know, then there was no chance that I would have a clue.

"We need to interview the parents," Conall said decisively.

"I'm sorry I couldn't get more."

Conall knelt in front of me. "You got us more than you think. This is what an investigation is like. Small frustrating pieces of information that point you in the right direction." He looked over at Flora. "I'm assuming you're going to the clinic again for any new patients."

Flora nodded.

Conall looked back at me. "When you've finished, I want you to come down to the Sheriff's office and watch the interviews. Maybe you'll see something that I can't."

I smiled at him, secretly pleased that he seemed to find my assistance valuable. "I'll be there."

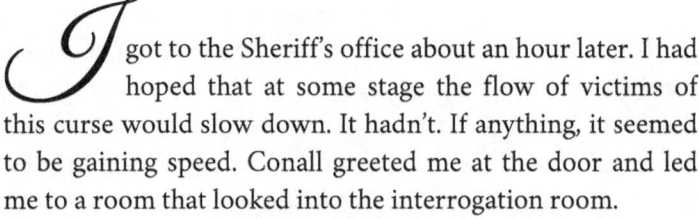

27

I got to the Sheriff's office about an hour later. I had hoped that at some stage the flow of victims of this curse would slow down. It hadn't. If anything, it seemed to be gaining speed. Conall greeted me at the door and led me to a room that looked into the interrogation room.

"I want you to sit here and just observe what these people are saying and doing. Maybe you'll pick up a clue that I'm missing." Conall hesitated before walking out. "Are you feeling up to this?"

I nodded wearily. "I'm fine. We need to get this done. The work I'm doing at the clinic is a bit wearing. The sooner we determine who's doing this, the sooner I can rest."

He stroked his thumb against my cheek, and I gave him a smile. "Go, do your thing. We'll get a chance to sort things out when this is finished."

After he left, I sat quietly in the observation room and closed my eyes, trying to allow some of the tension that had built up in me to seep away. I jumped when the door swung open.

"I've got the popcorn," Pike announced as he sat down next to me.

"Why would you bring popcorn?" I asked as I reached over for a handful.

"Because this is going to be the best show in town," he said with relish. "The Sheriff bringing in the alpha of the werewolf clan and the coven leaders of the Path Coven for questioning. I would pay to see this."

"Instead you're doing it for free as a babysitter," I said dryly, guessing the real reason for the deputy's company.

Pike smiled at me innocently. "You're a smart one. That's good. You'll keep the sheriff on his toes."

"How do you think this is going to play out?" I asked.

"I'm hoping for violence," Pike announced with relish.

Why was I not surprised? We stopped talking as Violet was brought into the interview room. She swept in as if she didn't have a care in the world. My interactions with Violet had mostly been brief, but I couldn't say that I was impressed with the woman. Flora cared deeply for her coven and hurt with every member in it. Violet seemed to care more for the position than for her coven.

"Take a seat." I winced at Conall's tone. Looked like somebody else had the position of good cop today. Following Violet into the interrogation room was one of the other deputies that I had met. I seemed to remember his name being Diaz. He was one of the werewolves who Conall had inherited when he became sheriff. If I was reading his body language correctly, he was not comfortable with today's activities. He sat down stiffly next to Conall, across from Violet.

"Did you wish to inform me why you dared to call me in here? I am sure that the Conclave would be very interested to know how I am being treated. You do remember that my son's father is a member of the Conclave."

Looked like Violet believed in a pre-emptive strike.

Conall leaned forward over the table. "Strange, I would have thought that as a loving mother, you would want to do anything that could help heal your son from his current affliction. Of course, if your maternal instincts aren't enough, his position as magister reflects well on you. Having him die would most likely hurt your ambition, wouldn't it?"

"I love my son," Violet said as if by rote with no real feeling behind the words.

"I doubt that very much," Conall shot back. "We have reason to believe that Magister Bernauer was deliberately infected with this disease. Do you have any idea who would do that?"

Violet shrugged. "My son is an important man. Important people make enemies. I'm sure there are any number of people who would have targeted him. I wouldn't know."

"Would your answer be any different if you found out that the other victims we believe were the main targets were Jim Greensmith and Eamon Tolan."

Violet frowned. "Are you sure?"

"Yes," Conall replied shortly.

I could see the agitation in Violet's expression. "I have no idea."

"Would there be any reason for you to target them?"

I glanced over at Pike to see him shoveling popcorn in his mouth and chuckling gleefully.

Violet spluttered. "How dare you?"

"That's not an answer," Conall said calmly.

"I would never target my own flesh and blood. I love my son with all my heart."

"Okay, that was a bit over the top," muttered Pike. "I'm pretty sure that woman would sell her heart for more power."

I nodded in agreement, but my concentration was completely taken with what was happening in front of me.

Conall leaned back in his seat. "My understanding is that you pretty much sold your son to his father when he was born, and that you're not particularly close. In fact, I have it on good authority that he describes you in the normal world as the stripper his father banged once when he was blind drunk."

I winced. I'd told him that.

I looked over as Pike laughed so hard he fell off the chair. Fortunately, I managed to save what was left of the popcorn just as it almost toppled over.

Violet drew herself up with frost emanating from her tone. "You are misinformed. My relationship with my son is a strong and loving one. If you are looking for someone who could be targeting him or me, maybe you should be looking at Flora Harstone and that insipid niece of hers.

"Insipid," I whispered in outrage. "Do you think I'm insipid?"

Pike screwed up his face. "I wouldn't call you insipid. More like vanilla."

"Why would you think I'm vanilla?"

Most people would have placated me at this point. I was beginning to learn that Pike was not most people.

"I'm just saying, if I had a coven leader and a berserker werewolf at my beck and call, I'd be using them a lot more creatively."

I was impressed that Conall didn't make one sign that the insult made him want to reach across the table and rip Violet's throat out.

"And why would you suggest that the most powerful witch in town and my Destined Beloved have decided to target you specifically, despite the fact they are almost killing themselves trying to keep people alive long enough for us to find the perpetrator of this crime?"

Nice. Conall had managed to insult Violet and remind her of what I was to him all in one tightly controlled statement.

Violet didn't get the hint and plowed on. "They're jealous that my coven is growing in power and theirs is stagnating. The day of reckoning is at hand."

Pike snorted and bits of popcorn sprayed out of his mouth. "She wishes."

"That's an interesting interpretation of the situation in this town," Conall commented. "It makes me wonder, what are you willing to sacrifice to ensure this future happens?"

"I won't have to sacrifice anything," Violet intoned ominously. "The future is already written. I just need to be patient."

"And we're headed into crazy town," Pike commented.

"Do you think she truly believes any of what she just said?" I had to admit it was a concerning look into her mind.

"I think she badly wants to believe that at some point she is going to be the preeminent witch in this town. She doesn't seem to realize that it's not just Flora's power that brings respect. Flora cares about the people in this town and she always has. Don't think that people haven't noticed that you and Flora have been at the clinic constantly. They've also noticed that people have stopped dying from this contagion since you started working with them. Most of this town has been affected in one way or another by what has been going on. That's a lot of goodwill that the Walker Coven has, and it has nothing to do with how much power they wield."

I didn't know how to respond to Pike's observations. It was probably very naive to imagine we could fly under the radar when dealing with something as big as this, but I had hoped not to attract too much attention.

Our focus was drawn back to the interrogation room when we heard the scraping of chairs as the sheriff and deputy stood up.

"Thank you for your assistance, Ms Hallybread. I will be contacting you if I have further questions."

The look Violet gave the two police officers was full of loathing, and I felt sorry for Deputy Diaz as he followed her out of the room.

Conall glanced up at the one-way window that we were using to watch the proceedings. "You do realize that I can hear the both of you. You might want to use that privacy spell of yours. I'd rather not be distracted when dealing with these people."

"Sorry," I mumbled as I reached into the bag and pulled out my cone of silence troll doll. I activated it and left it sitting on my lap.

Pike glanced down at the one pitiful example of my skills as a witch. "You're not a normal member of the coven, are you?"

"What gave it away?"

Pike smiled. "Most witches find image important. Like Violet and her Earth Mother schtick. It breeds a certain amount of conformity. You don't seem to fit with that."

"You might not want to mistake lack of ability with indi-viduality," I said as I reached for more popcorn.

"Maybe," he replied thoughtfully.

28

When Deputy Diaz returned to the interrogation room, he was followed by Elspeth Pickering who was only slightly less annoyed that she was called in than Violet had been.

"Is this going to take long, Sheriff. I have things to do."

"Would one of those things be visiting your son while he lies in a coma?" Conall asked smoothly.

"I have no son," Elspeth replied just as smoothly.

I winced at the series of colorful statements that Pike made describing the woman's character and parentage. It was a good thing I'd put on the privacy spell, because I had a feeling Conall would have had trouble ignoring those words.

"According to his birth certificate, Jim Greensmith was your son until he was fourteen years old and you abandoned him because he didn't fit into that cult you call a coven."

I could tell from Elspeth's expression that her mild dislike for the sheriff was now a raging case of hatred.

"The Path Coven is fulfilling our destiny. To do that we make sacrifices."

Conall jumped on that last statement. "How much of a sacrifice are you willing to make?"

For the first time Elspeth looked unsure of herself. "What exactly are you talking about?"

Conall looked down at the papers in his hand. "We have reason to believe that three of the men were the primary targets in this plague. Those men were Jim Greensmith, Julian Bernauer and Eamon Tolan."

"And what does that have to do with me?"

"There's a possibility that whoever did this made a sacrifice of their own son. With your lack of maternal feelings for Jim, you can understand why you would come under scrutiny."

"A sacrifice generally requires a loss. I would not consider his death a loss. He is nothing to me. And those other men mean less than nothing to me. As far as I am concerned, they are a drain on our power, and we are better off without them."

Conall looked at the woman with disgust. "You have what most of society would consider extremist views. Would you act on them and maybe thin the herd a little?"

"No, I would not. Men have their uses, as long as they are nowhere near the power of the coven."

Conall nodded. "That's it for now. I would suggest you don't go too far. I have a feeling that I'll have more questions for you very soon."

Elspeth nodded and left the room quickly.

"I couldn't read her," I complained. "I'm not sure whether she is hiding her feelings behind hateful language or whether she just doesn't care."

"I vote for not caring," Pike stated. "I've known Jim for years and that woman hasn't even looked in his direction in all that time. She is a cold, heartless, sorry excuse for a human being. Unfortunately, there have been too many members of the Path Coven who have bought into this whole males will weaken the power level propaganda. If it wasn't for the members of the Walker Bay Coven taking in these kids, I'm not sure where they would be."

I was surprised when Ilsa Hocking was brought into the interrogation room. "Why are they talking to her?"

"Just because she doesn't seem to have a link to this case, it's never a good idea to disregard her," Pike warned. "She's still a leader of the coven that believes men are a hindrance to attaining power. In her own way she is just as fanatical as Violet and Elspeth."

"Ms Hocking, thank you for agreeing to meet with us."

I was surprised by Conall's conciliatory approach compared to the way he had dealt with Violet and Elspeth. Then again, his brother had murdered her daughter. It wasn't exactly going to be a comfortable situation for either of them.

"We have discovered that three of the men who have been struck down by the disease going through the town have been hit harder than the others. It's as if they have been targeted. Those men are Julian Bernauer, Jim Green-smith and Eamon Tolan. We are trying to discover the reason why those men are different to the others, and whether that link can help us capture the person who has created this plague."

"And how do you think I can help," Ilsa asked frostily, her stiff countenance broadcasting her discomfort at the situation.

"Two of those victims are the sons of your co-leaders. It seems natural to assume that there is a possibility that your coven is being targeted."

"I doubt that," snapped Ilsa. "If we were being targeted it would be our daughters who would be falling prey to this illness. Not the sons we no longer want."

I glanced over at Pike. "Are you sure she doesn't have a son that she abandoned somewhere along the line?"

Pike shook his head. "Ilsa has lived in this town her entire life. She hasn't even left it for a holiday. In all that time, she has had one pregnancy and that produced Jeanette. Those words she's using are the same ones every member of the Path Coven uses whenever anyone questions them about the boys. The sheriff was right when he called the Path Coven a cult. Not politically astute, but he was right."

"Can you think of anyone with the will and capability of unleashing this plague on Walker Bay?"

"I would never presume to guess who is capable of this kind of magic," Ilsa replied. "And for the last few weeks I have been mourning the loss of my daughter at the hands of your brother. I have not had the time nor the inclination to evaluate anybody else's psychological state. I believe that is your job." She stood up and wiped her hands down the skirt of her black dress. "Now, if you no longer need to ask me questions about a situation which I have no interest in, I would like to leave."

Conall nodded shortly and Deputy Diaz departed with the clearly irritated woman.

Pike rubbed his hands together. "Okay we've had the undercard. Now it's time for the main event." He must have noticed my confusion. "Those are terms used for fighting matches. We are seriously going to have to broaden your education."

I really didn't like the way he said that. I caught my breath when Aidan Tolan swaggered in the room with Diaz following close behind.

As he sat down, I felt that now familiar pressure in my head. Deputy Diaz dropped his head, his body turning in on itself in his attempt to appear small. Pike groaned and dropped to the floor, his body shaking uncontrollably. I went to Pike, wishing I knew how to combat this dominance spell.

"Knock that off," Conall snapped, totally unaffected by the power play.

Even though he couldn't see me, I glared at the arrogant alpha. There would be nothing I'd enjoy more than wiping that smug look off Aidan's face when he used this particular spell.

Aidan gave Conall a grin. "Whatever you say, Sheriff," he spat.

The air suddenly seemed lighter. Diaz sat straighter, but I could see the anger in his eyes. It looked like not all were-wolves were enamored of their alpha. I helped Pike back in his chair.

He watched me in wonder. "I'd heard you and the Sheriff weren't affected by Aidan's dominance spell. I didn't quite believe it. Man, that must tick him off."

"I hope so," I replied, anger coursing through me at the pettiness of the man.

"Did you want to tell me why I am here?" Aidan asked, the boredom in his voice indicating how seriously he was taking this situation.

"You are here because we have reason to believe that Eamon was targeted by the plague that has been sweeping through town, along with Julian Bernauer and Jim Greensmith.

For the first time I saw a reaction from Aidan. He leaned forward. "Are you sure? What makes you think those three men have been targeted, considering over a hundred people have come down with this illness."

"The Walker Bay Coven has been treating the patients, and they have noticed a significant difference in the severity of the symptoms between the majority of patients and those three men. There is also the coincidence that they are the sons of the werewolf alpha and two of the Path Coven leaders. Can you think of any reason those three men would be targeted?"

"Power breeds jealousy from those who are weaker."

It was Conall's turn to be bored. "Cut the slogans. This is Eamon's life we're talking about. Now, either somebody we don't know about targeted those three, or you're behind this, and sacrificing Eamon is the price for your power."

For a split-second Aidan looked stunned at Conall's accusation. That didn't last long. "You are suggesting I deliberately infected my firstborn son and heir!" Aiden roared. "If I was inclined to kill one of my sons, it would have been the runt of the litter."

Conall didn't even flinch, which made me wonder how many times he had heard statements like that before.

"I'm going to need your stun gun." My voice vibrated with anger.

"Get in line," muttered Pike, his expression as dark as mine.

Seeing that he got no response from his son, Aidan changed tactics. "Exactly how do you suggest I accomplished this? It sounds like a spell or a potion, and I'm not a witch."

"This town is full of witches," Conall said calmly. "I'm sure one of them would be willing to do your bidding if they felt the reward was worth it."

"I don't consort with witches," Aidan spat.

Conall leaned back in his chair. "Really, that's interesting. What would you call your affair with Jeanette Hocking?"

Both Diaz and Pike started at that revelation.

"A lie made up by my enemies."

"I know you were sleeping with Jeanette."

"That's not true."

"I have your DNA on the sheets in the cottage as proof."

"You're lying."

I had to give Aidan some credit. He did not flinch in the face of Conall's accusations. If I hadn't known the truth, I would have believed him.

Conall leaned forward. "Ask your pet detective. I was the one that called her about the cottage. Before I did that and allowed her to corrupt the scene, I took my own forensic swabs, which means not all the evidence from the Jeanette Hocking murder was contaminated. Some of it is currently sitting somewhere very safe, waiting for the day when I choose to use it. Now, I would suggest that you become a great deal more forthcoming with me."

For the first time, I saw Aidan looking hesitant. I couldn't help but notice that both Diaz and Pike sat straighter at the sight.

I cursed when I felt my phone vibrating in my pocket. Planning to ignore it, I saw Flora's name flash up and knew I had to take it. Pike was so wrapped in the scene before him that he didn't even notice as I answered the phone.

Before I could speak Flora rushed ahead. "We've got another bad one." Her voice broke. "Sadie, it's a child."

I glanced back at the interview room where Conall was being frustrated at every turn by his father. Flora's statement blew our whole theory out of the water. "I need to go to the clinic," I whispered to Pike urgently. "When the sheriff is finished, let him know there's been another serious victim. All I know is he's a child."

Pike nodded. "I will." He looked back to where Conall was still grilling his father. "He's not going to be happy."

I had a feeling none of us were.

29

I raced up the steps at the clinic in an all too familiar way, only to meet Marigold at the reception desk.

"He's in here," she gasped with tears in her eyes. "Flora's doing all she can, but his parents were trying to heal him themselves. I don't know whether they got him here in time."

She ushered me into an examination room and I gasped in horror at the sight before me. A small figure lay on the bed, but it was impossible to tell what it was as the body was completely covered in a writhing mass of darkness. Flora looked up at me. "Thank goodness, I'm doing all I can, but I don't know if it's enough."

I strode up to the bed, determination flowing through me. I could almost feel the cursebreaker power sparking along my nerves.

"Everybody get out," Flora commanded, a small amount of her power pushing away any reluctance.

By the time the door slammed, I was already working.

"What happened? Why didn't anybody realize what was happening to this kid?"

"His parents don't like using outside medical intervention. They thought they could deal with it themselves."

I tamped down my irritation. Second guessing his parents was not going to help the situation here.

"How bad is it?" Flora asked, her voice subdued as she watched me feverishly plucking at something she couldn't see.

"It's so much worse than the others, I almost don't know where to begin," I said through gritted teeth.

Unlike before, I wasn't being delicate about this process. I was grabbing clumps of these things, but the amount just seemed to be never-ending. It was like the child had been mummified in the darkness. At this stage, I couldn't even see if he was still breathing, his whole face was covered in tendrils. As I finally managed to get away the last of the writhing mass that was clinging to his face, my heart broke at how gaunt this child seemed.

"Is he still breathing?" I asked desperately, unable to stop what I was doing to check.

Flora put her hand near his mouth.

"Yes, barely, but it's there." The relief in her voice was obvious to hear.

I doubled my efforts. By this time I was scraping the piles of tendrils away from the body. I figured I'd destroy those that survived my lack of care once I'd got them all off the boy.

The door opened behind me, but I refused to stop what I was doing. My fears of being discovered seemed to have faded in the face of what this child was going through. I felt a gentle hand against my back, and I knew that Conall had arrived and was trying to give me some of his strength.

An hour later the last of the tendrils had been destroyed. When I examined the child I felt like crying. He was desperately thin as if the darkness had been feeding off him. There was not an inch of his body that wasn't covered in angry welts. He looked to be only nine or ten, too young for the battle he'd found himself in the middle of.

"Are you okay?" murmured Conall.

I shook my head, afraid that if I answered I would burst into tears. Conall seemed to understand and he wrapped me in his arms. I drew in his strength for a few minutes as we listened to Flora working a soothing spell on the welts.

"What are you doing here?" I asked.

"I came here to tell you I'm executing search warrants on the houses of the Path Coven leaders and Aidan. I was wondering if you'd be willing to go with me."

"Sure, we just need to finish here first."

"No problem, I've got guards on each of the houses. Nobody's doing anything until we get there."

"Who have you got on Aidan's house?"

"Pike volunteered." Conall looked down at me with a wry smile. "He told me I wouldn't have to pay him overtime for a month if I let him have that detail."

When my aunt finished I drew in a deep breath and reluctantly stepped back.

"Looks like our theory got torpedoed."

"He doesn't seem to fit in with the other three, does he?" Conall looked over at Flora. "What do you know about the parents?"

"Calvin and Miriam Barr keep to themselves most of the time. They used to be very well known in town but about the time that Louis was born they cut themselves off and went off the grid for everything. They home school the child and they hardly come into town." She frowned as she looked over at the boy. "I'm surprised they took so long to bring Louis in. I've never known them to be that stubborn. It took them so long to have a child, I would have thought they'd be the kind of parents who took him to the doctor at the slightest sniffle."

"I'd better have a talk to them," Conall announced, kissing my cheek before he headed out the door.

"I'll go with you." Flora followed him. "They can be a little jittery sometimes. If I'm there they may be a little more forthcoming."

"I'll wait here," I said wearily as I dropped into a chair beside the bed. I pulled out a bottle of hand sanitizer I had decided to start carrying. I didn't know how much it helped, but it made me feel better.

"Who would do this to you?" I mused into the quiet room.

"Are you sure someone did this to him?"

I almost jumped out of my skin at the unexpected visitor. "Could you please not do that, Myra," I gasped, trying to slow my heartbeat down. "What are you doing in here?"

"He looks really bad," she said softly, her hand reaching out to comb some of the child's hair back.

"Do you know him?"

She shook her head hesitantly, but her eyes didn't leave his face as if she was searching for something.

"If you know something, Myra, you need to tell us. More people are going to die if we can't find out who did this."

"I don't know anything," Myra said, refusing to look at me.

"There are over a hundred people crammed into this clinic who have no quality of life at all," I said urgently. "That is not going to change unless somebody steps up and gives us something we can use."

"I don't know anything that's going to help," Myra replied.

"I don't think that's true," Conall's voice rumbled from the doorway. "For instance, I believe you delivered Louis to the Barrs on the day he was born and told them to keep him away from the people in town. You also told them that if anybody found out that he wasn't their child, that the outcome could be catastrophic."

Myra closed her eyes, a defeated expression crossing her face.

"Is he your child?" Conall asked roughly.

Myra shook her head. "No, he isn't my child."

I searched Louis's features. "He's Jeanette's child, isn't he?" My eyes searched out Conall's. "Ilsa's grandson."

Myra's face crumpled. "You can't tell her," she whispered. "I promised Jeanette her mother would never find out."

"Considering what happened to Jeanette, I would think her mother would be thrilled to learn there's a piece of her daughter still around."

Myra laughed without any humor. "You'd think so, wouldn't you? If it had been a girl, that would have been true. She would have been shocked. Jeanette was only eighteen when she got pregnant. But she would have welcomed a girl."

"But not a boy," I murmured.

"Ilsa has a very firm belief system," Myra replied.

"Who was the father?" I refused to look at Conall. I knew he and Jeanette were together briefly when they were teenagers. I just didn't know the timing.

"Jeanette went through a bit of a wild time when Conall left town. She never knew exactly who the father was, just that he was a witch."

"How did you hide it?" Conall asked. "I've never even heard a whisper of Jeanette being pregnant."

"Girls have been doing it for centuries. It wasn't particularly difficult." She looked up at Conall. "We were worried about how Ilsa would have reacted if she discovered Jeanette had a son. She hasn't been entirely stable for a while."

"What do you mean, 'not entirely stable'?" I asked.

"It was Jeanette's grandmother who was the driving force

behind us becoming a part of the Path Coven. She firmly believed that the coven would only be powerful if it wasn't diluted by males. She even believed that any male babies should be sacrificed at birth, for the good of the coven. She toned down the rhetoric in public, but her private views were well known, and Ilsa shared them."

"You and Jeanette were trying to protect the boy." I looked down at the child in question. I couldn't even begin to understand the kind of fanaticism Myra was talking about.

"Is there a chance that Ilsa knows about the boy?" Conall asked.

Myra shook her head. "I told the Barrs to keep him out of town, away from everybody. She wouldn't have even seen him." She looked down at Louis again and shook her head. "I came to visit my brother. I shouldn't even be here. He's the Barr's son now." She looked up again. "Please don't tell anybody. Jeanette never wanted anyone to find out."

I studied the young boy that was near death. "I have a bad feeling somebody already knows."

"What do you think?" Conall asked after Myra had left the room.

"I think our theory just got strengthened. Ilsa's firstborn grandson just rounded out the entire coven leadership group."

"And don't forget the werewolf alpha," Conall sighed.

"I doubt I ever could." I frowned. "He does seem to be a bit of an anomaly, doesn't he? I mean, why Aidan and not one of the other members of the Council? Do any of them have firstborn sons?"

"Both Dorota and Cary do."

"I wouldn't know whether either of their sons are among the patients, but I do know that they aren't the ones with the super strain of whatever this is."

"So, it isn't a power play against the Council." Conall glanced up at me.

I nodded. "He was worse than the other three. I don't know whether it was because his parents took too long before they got him medical attention, or whether there's another reason. I do think we might want to execute the search warrants starting with Ilsa."

Conall grimaced as he watched the small boy struggling to breathe. "I think you're right."

30

*I*lsa's house was easy to find, despite being back from the road on the outskirts of town.

"Is that black fabric hanging off the front of her house?"

Conall nodded grimly. "Jeanette was her only child. Some of the families use very old traditions to mourn the death of their loved ones."

"I can't imagine the pain she's going through," I murmured.

"Grief can make people do crazy things. I need you here because you're the only one who can see those tendrils you talk about. If the curse tablet is hidden anywhere around here, you've got the best chance of seeing it. If we don't find anything, we'll move on to Violet's place."

When we got out of the car, I frowned as I looked around. "I thought you said you had deputies on each of the properties."

"I did."

"Then, where are they?"

"I don't know," he said slowly. "I think it might be a good idea if you wait in the car."

"Did I ever tell you about the curse Jeanette had put around the cottage where she and your father were having their affair?"

"No, I'm assuming you have a point."

"It was designed to make people go mad the second they crossed it. Tilda came within two feet of it before I stopped her. She didn't see it and she wouldn't have even known what happened to her. I'm thinking a berserker sheriff going insane is the last thing this town needs."

"Fine, your point is made, but if I tell you to run, you are to obey without question."

"Whatever you say."

We approached the house and were surprised to find the front door wide open. I could see Conall was nervous, and I was pretty sure I knew the reason why.

"Stop worrying about me and focus on how you would normally do your job. Trust me, if things get hairy, I'm letting you take care of it."

Conall nodded, but I could see his attention was still torn. We entered the house carefully and I gasped at what we found in the front room. Two of Conall's deputies were encased in crystal, similar to how I'd found Myra once when she broke into my house.

"They must have crossed some of her wards," I said as I tapped on the crystal. "I've seen this before. Flora uses the same kind of wards on my house. Goes off instantly if somebody breaks in. She might be able to help get them out." I studied the two deputies. "Why aren't we affected by the wards?"

"Usually the reason would be because all wards are supposed to include exemptions for emergency responders, and because you came with me you would be safe." He gestured towards the two deputies. "In this case I would suggest that doesn't apply.

The other alternative is that it takes a certain amount of strength to maintain wards on a property. They're not something you can set and forget. Maybe she needs the strength elsewhere, so she pulled them off after the deputies came in."

"That doesn't sound good."

"I never claimed it was a good thing."

I looked around the house. "Is Ilsa always this messy?"

"I wouldn't have thought so." Conall stepped over some papers that were on the ground and his shoes crunched on what sounded like broken glass. "I've got a very bad feeling about this."

"We might want to check out the basement," I looked around to see if I could find the way. "It seems that everything bad in this town always begins in a basement."

"That's witches for you," muttered Conall.

When we finally located the door to the basement, I was only too happy to let Conall take the lead. Rickety steps leading down to a dark basement was a little too close to a horror movie for me to try being brave. As we made our way down, we could hear a voice rising in tempo. It stopped as we hit the bottom step.

"Sheriff, I was expecting you." She glanced dismissively in my direction. "I shouldn't be surprised to see your pet with you."

I was getting a little tired of the whole witch and werewolf insults that kept flying around.

"What are you doing, Ilsa?" Conall asked conversationally.

"I'm righting a wrong, one that you should have taken care of."

My mind flew to the only wrong that I could think of. "The sheriff put Brian behind bars for killing Jeanette."

Ilsa snorted derisively. "That animal may have been the

weapon, but the ones behind her death are the ones who haven't been punished."

"Why do you think the whole town needs to be punished for Jeanette's death?" I persisted. I could see Conall wasn't happy with the way I was asking questions, but I needed to understand why someone would commit mass murder of innocents just to target a few.

"The werewolf alpha ordered the death of my baby," she spat.

"Do you have proof?" Conall leaned forward with interest. "If you have proof Aidan was behind Jeanette's death, I will arrest him in a heartbeat."

She shook her head. "I don't need proof. I know he did it. He found out what she was doing."

"What was she doing?" I didn't think Conall wanted the answer to the next part of his question.

"She was going to be the wife of the werewolf alpha. She would have had complete control over the entire clan, the first witch with that power in hundreds of years."

Conall shook his head. "That was never going to happen. Aidan might have had a fling with Jeanette, but he would never put a witch in that position of power."

Ilsa smiled grimly. "Yes, he would have. We only needed a little more time before he was under our sway."

Conall paled. "You were trying to put a hex mark on Aidan."

"You're quick for a werewolf."

"What's a hex mark?" I hated the way I always seemed to be catching up on any conversation in this town.

Ilsa smiled indulgently. "A way to keep werewolves in their place."

Conall snarled. "It's a curse that was purged centuries ago. It's a brand with a curse behind it that turns werewolves into mindless slaves. It's how witches kept us under control for so long."

We finally had the answer to why Aidan had wanted Jeanette killed. Her life would have been forfeit the second he found out she was trying to enslave the clan using him. "You think Violet and Elspeth told Aidan what Jeanette was doing?"

"They didn't agree. They thought we should wait for our moment. They didn't understand the moment is now. The prophecy is now."

"What prophecy?" I couldn't stop the frustration in my voice. All we kept getting were little pieces of information.

"When we will take our rightful place in the world. I am to be one of the Triumvirate. It has been promised."

"Was it worth sacrificing your grandson?" Of all her sins, to me, that seemed to be the worst.

"Yes." Ilsa didn't even falter.

"Jeanette cared about that boy. She tried to protect him from you."

Ilsa smiled grimly. "I always knew about the boy. She should have known better than to try to hide him. I knew one day I'd need a sacrifice to increase my power, and she provided one for me. I just needed to wait for the right time."

She raised her hands in the air and I felt wind swirling around us. I glanced at Conall and saw he agreed with me. This was not good.

"You are in our way, Sheriff. A Destined Beloved prophecy between a werewolf and a witch is considered an abomination. It can't be allowed to stand."

She pulled out a knife and drew it across the palm of her hand. I watched, fascinated, as she squeezed her fist tightly and drops of blood fell to the floor. She stepped back and I saw the stone tablet which had been hidden beneath her long skirt. The blood dripped on the tablet and I could hear the sizzle. Words started screeching in my mind. I could see what the curse wanted, and I was not going to let it happen. With every bit of strength in my body, I pushed an unsuspecting Conall to the side, just as Ilsa released the curse that was aimed solely at destroying the man I was beginning to realize that I was falling in love with.

For the second time in my life I put myself in the path of a fatal curse and hoped that I was strong enough to withstand it. I felt it hit me and bounce off. Images streaked through my mind of Ilsa's ambitions, of her hatred for everyone after her daughter died, and of her desperate desire for revenge on those she blamed, regardless of their guilt. I also felt the curse's frustration at not being able to fulfill its goal. Flora and I were right when we talked about a curse being almost sentient, and it seemed I was growing strong enough to read them. Unable to go anywhere else it was pulled back to Ilsa, like it was connected by a bungee rope. I felt it hit her and spread across her body. Unlike the curse she had aimed at the town, this one had a strength and a hunger that was instantaneous. There was no slow build up. The tendrils immediately covered her whole body. I ran to Ilsa, scooped up the tablet and flung it at the floor. Surprisingly, it smashed on impact. I had always thought I needed to get rid of the tendrils before I could do that. When I looked around at Ilsa, I saw why this time was different. The tendrils had disintegrated at the same time as the tablet, leaving a desiccated corpse in their wake. She had been dead before I smashed the tablet. I was going to need to remember that in the future. It was obvious she had used a far stronger curse this time. If she'd unleashed this one on the town, there would have been carnage.

I barely had time to think about that when I was grabbed from behind and spun around.

"Are you out of your mind?" Conall snarled. "You are never to put yourself in front of me when we are in danger. I don't care about your abilities. You are never to even think of sacrificing yourself for me."

I had seen Conall angry before, but I don't think I'd ever seen him quite this furious. While he was still ranting I placed my hands on the sides of his face and reached up to press my lips against his. He froze, and then must have realized that this was the first time that I had initiated a kiss. Before he could take the kiss deeper, I pulled back and smiled at the heat I could see in his eyes.

"I choose you," I whispered.

When I realized the curse Ilsa was creating was aimed at Conall, I had never felt such fear in my life. The thought of losing him had almost paralyzed me.

The smile that crossed Conall's face was blinding. "I'm glad you caught up, I chose you a long time ago."

31

*W*hen Conall and I went back upstairs, we found the two deputies, lying on the floor groaning. Flora had told me that one of the biggest differences between spells and curses was that a spell could be nullified by a witch's death. Unfortunately, curses could last forever.

I helped the one who looked lighter to his feet. "We should probably get them checked out."

We bundled the two deputies into Conall's truck and headed back to the clinic which, as was usual these days, was packed to capacity. The deputies were going to be waiting for a while.

After Conall had ordered his two deputies to get a clean bill of health from the doctor before they were permitted to go back to work, he found me in the doorway of Louis's room.

"I hoped that this would all be over with when Ilsa died."

I pushed myself up from the door frame. "Not yet, but it will be soon."

Conall followed me as I left the clinic. "Where are we going."

Knowing this was a conversation that I really didn't want anybody to hear, I activated my troll doll. "Ilsa did this as revenge for Jeanette's murder, so it's logical that she would hide the curse tablet somewhere related to Jeanette's death."

"You think it's where we found Jeanette's body," he concluded.

"I think it's as good a place as any to start."

The drive to the park that overlooked the bay wasn't far. I was surprised to see how deserted the streets were. "Where is everyone?"

"Nobody knows where this plague is coming from, and almost all the families have been hit in some way." Conall replied. "Everyone who can is staying inside in case it's airborne."

When we reached the park it didn't take me long to discover I had been right. "It's here."

The bench where I had enjoyed some beautiful sunrises coming up over the bay was now covered in the dark tendrils that had become such a fixture of my life. The darkness covered the seat and draped over the edges like a waterfall, and when they hit the ground, they spread into two mounds. I went to work clearing them away from the bench.

Conall took up a position that would allow him to see if anybody approached. "I don't like this. It's too open."

"I don't have much choice," I muttered. "This is where she did the curse, the same place where Brian murdered her daughter." I looked up at Conall. "I thought this was a nice quiet town where people got along with each other."

Conall sighed and raked his hand through his hair. "For the most part it is, but no society is perfect. Nothing can take away from the resentment and fear that some werewolves feel towards witches, or the sense of entitlement that some witches have over werewolves. We're not even going to go into the problems between the trolls and the ogres. There's so much history between the races. We try to get along, but there are some pockets who want a return to the old ways. I'm afraid that's what this prophecy is about." He looked around, concern etched into his features. "Please hurry up. I really don't like this. Anyone can see what you're doing."

"I'm doing the best I can," I said through gritted teeth. "This isn't the most pleasant job in the world. Believe me when I say I'd prefer to have the weather power that Tilda's grandmother has."

"We'd all prefer to have that one," Conall grunted.

I finished destroying the tendrils and eyed two mounds of dirt on either side of the bench. "I need something to dig with."

Conall instantly reached down into his boot and removed a knife.

"I'm assuming this isn't standard equipment for a sheriff."

"It should be," Conall replied. "You wouldn't believe how many times that knife has saved my hide."

I started digging at the ground.

Conall knelt down beside me and held out his hand. "I'll do that, just tell me where to dig."

I shook my head. "No, I need to do this. You need to keep watch. I don't want to have an angry mob after me, just because somebody decided that they were brave or stupid enough to walk their dog despite the plague."

Conall resumed his watch. It didn't take long for me to feel metal meeting stone. I scraped away the dirt and levered the tablet out. Instantly, I was overwhelmed by those seductive whispers. My first instinct was to destroy the thing, but I wanted to know what was under the other mound. I set the tablet aside and started digging again. Now that I knew what I was looking for, it didn't take long for me to once again feel the knife meeting the stone. When I got the second tablet out the whispering grew louder. I was being promised everything I could possibly want. I fought against the twin temptations. The first to destroy the tablets immediately. The second to know what was on them. All these curses happening in Walker Bay weren't a coincidence, and I had a feeling that they weren't going to stop. Somebody else was behind all this and I had to find out who it was.

I sat cross legged on the ground figuring if I was going to collapse again, I wanted the fall to be as short as possible. I was practical that way. I held the tablets up and started reading what they were saying. The hate and prejudice that was coming off the stones in waves made me feel sick. If nothing else convinced me of Ilsa's evil, these tablets did. I'd had pretty harsh feelings about Jeanette ever since I'd found she'd put a curse around a cottage to protect her affair, with no thought of the innocents that could be harmed by it. Feeling Ilsa's hatred made me realize that Jeanette never stood a chance. The fact she'd allowed her son to survive, and even tried to protect him from her mother, redeemed her slightly in my eyes, but not much.

As I read the tablets, images and feelings came at me thick and fast. The most frustrating part was that I could feel that somebody had provided Ilsa and Jeanette with the curses and the power to cast those curses, but I couldn't see who it was. They were like a shadowy figure in the background, manipulating things but never coming into the light. Their power gave them voice and that voice was meant to tempt me. I gripped the tablets and held them as high above my head as I could. Once again, the voices offering temptation turned to ones screaming retribution. At the point where the tablets hit the ground and disintegrated into dust, a pain gripped my head and I slumped to the side.

32

I had to admit that wading to consciousness with Conall's arms wrapped around me was definitely one of the better things that had happened to me recently. I smiled up at him.

"Does it always kick your butt like that?"

I struggled to sit up as I realized this wasn't the romantic scenario that I thought it was. "It has the last couple of times. I think whoever created these ones is very experienced and has been doing it for a long time. The curse Isobel cast was more benign, maybe because it was the first, or because Isobel had a part in crafting it. I'm just lucky I ran into her first. If I'd faced one of these the first time, I'm not sure I would have been able to do anything."

"I don't ever want you facing one of these without me," he ordered.

I choked on a laugh. "Good luck with that. By the way, if you think ordering me around is going to work, you are in for a huge disappointment."

"I figured." Conall pulled himself up and then hauled me

to my feet with very little effort at all. "Are you able to make it back to the truck or do I need to carry you?"

I didn't even bother to respond as I walked ahead of him. When we arrived at the clinic it was in pandemonium. Families were crying and patients were up and walking around.

I followed Conall to his brother's room. When he saw Eamon sitting up, he strode to his side and hugged him. Eamon caught my eye over his brother's shoulder, and I could see the question in his eyes. I shook my head slightly. I would never tell anyone about his feelings for Tilda.

I started at the gentle touch of a hand on my shoulder and turned around.

"You look terrible."

"Thanks, Flora. That's just what I needed to hear after the day I've had."

My aunt smiled. "You know I don't mean that in a harsh way. I'm just worried about you. This whole situation has drained you." She looked over at the two brothers. "They started waking up about fifteen minutes ago."

That sounded about right.

"Ilsa was behind it," Conall informed her as he walked towards us. "She was looking for revenge for Jeanette's death."

"Is she...?"

I nodded. "She got caught trying to cast another one. A more potent one."

Flora shook her head sorrowfully. "How are so many falling from the path?"

I really didn't know the answer to that question. "The important thing is that Louis is safe now. His parents no longer need to be afraid. They can live a normal life. Maybe he could even go to school and have some friends."

Flora smiled gently. "I'll suggest it might be best for his social development, now that the danger is gone."

We were interrupted by an annoyed looking Violet and Myra.

"He wishes to speak to you."

I didn't have to ask who I was being summonsed by. I put a hand on Conall's arm. "I'll be right back."

When I entered Julian's room it was to find him already dressed and ready to leave.

"How are you feeling?"

"Was it a curse?" he barked.

It looked like we weren't bothering with niceties. I nodded.

"Who?"

"Ilsa Hocking. She wanted revenge against the town for the death of her daughter."

Julian frowned in confusion. "How was the town to blame?"

I shrugged. "I have no idea. She wasn't exactly firing on all cylinders."

"Is she dead?"

"Yes, she tried to cast a stronger curse when this one didn't seem to be effective enough. It backfired."

"Are you sure that's what happened?" Julian watched me keenly, and I had to admit it was a little concerning that he wasn't just accepting what I said. It wasn't surprising, he was a magister, after all.

"That's what I saw. The sheriff was with me. He might have more information if you want to talk to him."

An unpleasant look crossed Julian's face. "Of course, he was."

There was an uncomfortable silence while Julian watched me as if searching for something.

"Everything okay in here?"

I was surprised Conall had lasted this long.

Julian smiled and lifted his eyes. "I was just talking to

Sadie about Ilsa Hocking. A surprise that a respected coven leader would commit such a heinous act. I look forward to reading your report."

Conall's eyes narrowed. "I don't report to you."

Julian smiled again and I had no doubt he was going to get a copy of that report. "I see the situation in this town is more dire than I originally believed. We may be working closely together in the near future."

While his words were aimed at Conall, I was uncomfortably aware that his gaze was directed at me.

I suppressed a shiver that was only warmed when Conall put his arm around me in a clear signal to Julian to back off. "If you have any more dealings in this town, I would suggest you contact me," Conall said. "In the meantime, I believe your fiancée is waiting for you."

Julian grimaced at the pointed reminder of his pending marital status. "I'll be seeing you soon, Sadie."

We watched him leave.

"I really don't like him."

I laughed at the grumpiness in Conall's voice. "Really? I would never have guessed. You hide it so well."

I felt Conall's arm tighten around me. "I think he's going to be a problem."

I tipped my head up to look at him and saw the worry in his eyes. "Do you mean personally or professionally?"

"Both."

I leaned into the man I knew would always be there for me. I was afraid he was right.

ABOUT THE AUTHOR

Leonie Gant started her writing career at the age of ten when she stuffed notes in her pencil case full of ideas for mysteries that Nancy Drew and the Hardy Boys should really have been solving. After years of watching mysteries play out in her head she decided that writing them down was the best way to deal with them.

In her life away from writing, she is a voracious reader with not nearly enough time to make her way through all the books she wants to read. She enjoys bushwalking, sewing and chocolate, possibly not in that order.

To find out more about Leonie Gant and her books

www.leoniegant.com